# DRAGON SHIELD 3

**Also by Charlie Fletcher:**

Dragon Shield
Dragon Shield: The London Pride

Stoneheart
Ironhand
Silvertongue

Far Rockaway

# DRAGON SHIELD 3

## THE CITY OF BEASTS

### CHARLIE FLETCHER

*Illustrated by Nick Tankard*

*Hodder
Children's
Books*

Hodder Children's Books
First published in Great Britain in 2016 by Hodder and Stoughton

1 3 5 9 10 8 6 4 2

A CIP catalogue record for this book is available from the British Library

ISBN 978 1 444 91738 3

Typeset in Garamond by Avon DataSet Ltd,
Bidford-on-Avon, Warwickshire

Printed and bound in Great Britain by Clays Ltd, St Ives plc

The paper and board used in this book are from well-managed forests
and other responsible sources.

Hodder Children's Books
An imprint of Hachette Children's Group
Part of Hodder & Stoughton
Carmelite House
50 Victoria Embankment
London EC4Y 0DZ

An Hachette UK Company
www.hachette.co.uk

www.hachettechildrens.co.uk

# The story so far . . .

In the British Museum the curators have made a terrible mistake. They have mended an ancient sarcophagus, unknowingly joining up a broken band of hieroglyphics that has rekindled an ancient power, freeing the Egyptian god Bast from millennia of imprisonment inside a small bronze statue of a cat.

Bast has frozen time in the city and is determined to avenge herself on humankind.

In this layer of London the statues are alive and able to move, unseen by the inhabitants of the city.

The soldier-statues of the city have already tried to storm the museum and defeat Bast. Bast has cursed them into immobility for their insolence. Now Bast has also imprisoned the Temple Bar dragon and enslaved all the other statues of city dragons to her will. She has begun to assemble an army of all the animal statues in London.

Only two young humans can still move: Will and Jo, a brother and sister. They are accidentally protected from the curse by the scarab bracelets they were given by their mother. They are the city's last hope. They have help from the remaining non-military statues who are not frozen, and are travelling with a mismatched gang of them, but their plans have just met a nasty setback.

They had hoped to find their frozen mother where they left her in Coram's Fields. She had a third scarab bracelet on a key ring in her wallet. They'd planned to use this to start fighting back. They found the wallet. They used the scarab to break Bast's spell on a dragon that had been attacking them until it was made to, er, backfire by the gorilla statue that accompanies them.

But their mother is gone . . .

# 1

## *The Wild Idea*

Coram's Fields was full of blue-tinged frozen people and unmoving vehicles now seemingly forever trapped in a freeze-frame. Despite the crowd, and even though they were in the middle of the gang of statues that had come with them – a little girl, an impish boy, a young violinist, two leopards and a gorilla – faced by the empty spot that should have held their mother, Will and Jo had never felt more alone.

Will stared around at the façades of the blank houses facing the leafy square, with its knobbly trunked trees overhanging the tall iron railings.

'So what do we do now?' said Jo.

Will looked at her. She was scanning the rooftops around them and seemed exhausted and worried, and – from the way she was leaning on her stick – as if her bad knee was giving her trouble. That wouldn't be surprising, given the amount of running they'd had to do to escape from the nightmares that had been chasing them through the frozen horror-show that London had become. She caught him looking at her and took her weight off the stick. He pointed at the bench in the bus stop behind her.

'Hey, you should—'

'It's fine,' she said, cutting him off before he could get the suggestion out. She didn't like to talk about her knee, and she hated him making a fuss of her. She tried for a grin and nearly made it. 'So, seriously, what is your wild idea exactly?'

He thought her half-grin, in the circumstances, made her look about a hundred times tougher than he was feeling. He tried to sound confident.

'Find Mum,' he said. 'Find Mum and then . . .'

'Yup,' said Jo. And then she exhaled with an unmistakable puff of disappointment, her shoulders slumping as she did so. 'That's obvious. I mean, that's not a *wild* plan, is it? That's just what we have to do, that's our job. I thought you had a plan that might actually give us a chance of succeeding . . .'

The other thing that Will thought was extraordinary – given what they'd just been through together – was how irritating she could still be. The whole brother/ sister thing was clearly bombproof. He'd been about to tell her, and then she'd interrupted, and what had seemed like a good – if wild – plan a moment ago now shrivelled a bit in his head.

'Don't—' he began, then stopped himself. This wasn't the time for arguing.

'Don't what?' she said.

Will wished he had a better answer than a shrug, but he didn't. In fact, even his shrug now seemed a bit half-hearted.

Jo pointed around the street, at the unmoving people, the static cars and the empty space on the tarmac where they had last seen their mother.

'Don't go all grumpy now,' she said. 'We haven't got time for getting huffy with each other. I mean, in case you hadn't noticed, London's still frozen, except for the statues, who can move because of course *that* makes sense. Not. Oh, except the *soldier*-statues, of course, the ones who might actually have been able to help us fight the, the whatever . . .'

'Bast,' said Will, watching her looking at the rooftops as if she expected something bad to leap down on them at any minute.

'The cat in the museum,' said Jo. 'The one that thinks she's a god. So, the soldiers who might actually be good in a fight are frozen as still as the people. The animal statues are on the move and seem to be under the cat's power, as are the dragon statues, and all we have is . . .'

She turned round and looked at their companions. The two bronze boys, Wolfie and Tragedy, stood side by side, one splendid in an eighteenth-century coat and a wig, the other more of a tousle-haired street urchin. Both grinned hopefully back at her.

'A boy with a violin . . .' she said.

'A *wunderkind*, if you please!' said Wolfie. 'Not a boy. A *wunderkind*!'

And as if to prove the truth of his words he sawed at his violin, sending a trilling flourish of rising notes up into the empty sky above them. Tragedy grimaced and stuck his fingers in his ears.

'Shhh, Wolfie!' he hissed. 'You'll have them coming to see what that bleedin' racket is, you big show-off, and then we'll be in trouble, you see if we ain't!'

Wolfie frowned and put his hands on the strings to stop the sound. Jo pointed at the others standing around them. Next to Tragedy was a smiling statue of a little girl, who was stroking the back of one of the three animal statues that accompanied her wherever she went.

'We've got Tragedy, and Happy with her two cheetahs, and Guy the Gorilla and, I dunno . . .'

6

She nodded at a shamefaced silver-painted dragon sitting in a puddle that was still steaming from the heat of its submerged bottom.

'. . . Farty the dragon over there.'

The dragon's ears had been flattened back against its head with embarrassment, but they now pricked up sharply at her words.

'Oook,' he said, and tapped his chest with one large stabby talon. 'Oooky-ook-Oook?'

Jo shot a glance at Will, who just shrugged again. He had no idea why the dragon was looking suddenly and a bit unexpectedly pleased.

'Oh no,' said Tragedy, rolling his eyes. 'Now you been and gone and done it.'

'Done what?' said Jo.

'Oooky-ook-Oook,' repeated the dragon, waddling back out of the puddle and shaking like a dog coming out of the water. He pointed at Jo and then – keeping a nervous eye on Guy the Gorilla – took a step forward and tapped his chest self-importantly.

'You only give it a name, didn't you?' sighed Tragedy.

'It's never had a name before,' explained Happy.

'Oooky-ook-Oook!' said the dragon, nodding.

'Farty-the-Dragon,' said Tragedy. 'Got a ring to it,

I suppose. But now it thinks it's something special, see? Now it thinks you and it are related or something.'

'Is it on our side then?' said Will. 'Because I don't trust it and— What?'

Jo was turning in a fast circle, as if she had suddenly forgotten something and was looking for it.

'Where's Ariel?' she said.

He scanned the square and the sky above.

'She was here a moment ago,' he said.

'She comes and goes like that,' said Tragedy. 'Flits here and there without a by-your-leave.'

'She can be very abrupt,' said Wolfie, nodding. 'It can be very dizconzertink.'

'She's just a spirit of air,' said Happy, as if that explained everything. 'Being flighty? It's her nature. She'll be back in a jiffy, I expect.'

'Yeah,' said Tragedy, not sounding half as cheery and optimistic as the small girl, who was now walking towards the dragon. She did look *very* little and vulnerable next to the big silver lizard, but Guy knuckled along behind her like an ominous thundercloud, his eyes steady and locked on the reptile's every movement. Happy smiled up into the dragon's eyes and spoke so softly that they couldn't hear her words. The only part of the conversation they could get was the excited tumble of 'ooks' that spilled out of the creature's mouth in response.

'She understands all animals,' said Tragedy quietly, sidling up to Jo and Will.

'She's very brave,' said Jo.

'Farty's dead terrified of that gorilla,' said Tragedy, 'after what he done to him. It's like he broke him a bit.'

'Are we really calling him Farty now?' said Will. 'Really?'

'He likes it,' said Happy, turning towards them. 'I mean, he doesn't know what it means, but he likes it.'

'But is he on our side?' said Will. 'Just like that?'

'Well,' said Happy, putting her head on one side. 'Having his poor bottom turned into an unexpected flamethrower was a bit of a surprise moment for him, but you putting the scarab on him and lifting the spell was a bigger thing. And the biggest thing of all is what he saw in the museum! He saw that the Temple Bar dragon has been taken prisoner by Bast the cat.'

'Ah,' said Tragedy, nodding. 'That's like the cat taking your mum prisoner. Temple Bar's the top banana of all the dragons, just like a dad to 'em all.'

'And that is precisely what has happened to your mother, I'm afraid, as it turns out,' said Happy. 'I'm very sorry to tell you, and he is even more sorry now that he did it, but he told Bast about her and in fact led the very Sphinx here that has taken her.'

'Sphinx?' said Jo. 'What Sphinx?'

'What does it matter?' said Will, sitting down. 'Who or whatever took her, she's in the museum. It's just what I was worried about.'

'Oh, I didn't know you were actually *worried*!' said Jo. 'I thought you just had a wild and clever idea that was going to help rescue her!'

And here they were, as always, arguing at just the wrong time. He took a breath. Then another.

'My plan, if you want to know, is to take the spare scarab bracelet and use it to free as many of the soldier-statues as we can, and then fight our way into the museum and let them sort the cat out for us,' said Will. 'I mean, if it lifted the spell from the dragon, it'll lift the spell from them. It stands to reason.'

'Nothing about this has to do with reason,' said Jo. 'But you know what?'

He waited for her to pour cold water on what was, he knew, a bit more of a desperate hope than a real plan.

Then she grinned, full on this time.

'That might be genius!'

He felt a flush of relief go through his system.

'Well,' he said, returning her grin with a smile of his own. 'It might work, mightn't it?'

She nodded.

'It's a first step,' she said. And he knew just what she meant. It was something their dad used to say, half joking, half serious, an old Chinese proverb: *A journey of a thousand miles begins with a first step*. It really meant the best way to get anything unpleasant done was to simply do something, not to stay frozen just *thinking* about doing something. Especially when you're scared. Doing's a kind of fear-killer all by itself, he would say.

'Right,' Will said. 'Let's start with the Fusilier. Come on, everyone.'

He was so excited by the idea of being able to free the tough World War One statue who had sacrificed himself to save Will from certain death by dragon fire that he was already starting to jog off in the direction of Holborn before he saw them.

And then he felt Guy's hand fall on his shoulder like a shovel and grip him, stopping him dead in his tracks.

'Oook ook, oook!' hooted Farty from behind him.

Will didn't speak Dragon, but he knew what he was saying. He was saying 'Look out – lions!'

Because that's what was all around them, padding silently, confidently into the square from all the surrounding streets: more lions. Granite lions, Portland stone lions, bronze lions, marble lions and gilded lions, big lions, small lions, heraldic lions, life-sized lions and giant lions, lions in all shapes and sizes; what, in fact, looked like every lion statue in the city.

'The London Pride,' breathed Tragedy.

Will found he was standing with his arm round Jo and that even more surprisingly she wasn't squirming free as she normally did.

He felt her shiver.

'Will,' she said.

'I know,' he replied.

'Me too,' said Tragedy, gulping. 'We're kippered.'

# 2

## *Plan G*

That old Chinese proverb might be have been right in saying that a journey of a thousand miles begins with a single step, but it turned out not to be very helpful about how to proceed if your legs had just been kicked out from under you.

That's what Jo felt like as she watched the lions of the London Pride spill into the square all round them. She felt flattened and winded and, for the moment, unable to think, let alone move. Will had picked up the dragon shield and held it in front of them. Tragedy pulled Happy in behind it, and Wolfie stepped in behind her. Guy the Gorilla and the cheetahs made up the outer ring of defence, but the truth was that they were surrounded.

It wasn't that the lions moved especially fast. It was that they flowed relentlessly into position without needing to hurry, somehow as inevitable and unstoppable as the tide. It was something to do with the lazy, hypnotic swagger with which they stalked through the frozen pedestrians and unmoving cars. They moved as if they owned the city, as if this was their natural hunting ground, and they had such dangerous grace as they did so that it was impossible not to stop and watch in horrid fascination, a fascination made all the worse by the fact that the lions' eyes were all staring right back with a cold, predatory concentration of their own.

Multiply the brain-freezing intensity of that gaze by the hundred or so pairs of eyes that were sinuously moving into position all around them, and by the time all the various bits of you that should already be long gone untangled from the fear and got organised enough to start running for your life, it was already too late.

'We'd have a better chance inside,' said Will, staring around for a good line of escape.

'Oook,' squeaked the dragon, stepping outside the ring of defence to quickly pick up the battered plywood shield-shaped placard with GOLF SALE splashed across it and then jump back to safety.

'Too late,' said Jo. 'We'd never make it.'

Will nodded.

'I know.'

The lions were all round them now, and even the closest houses were too far away for them to have a chance of getting to safety before being taken down by the big hunting cats.

Jo looked down at Happy. The little girl looked back at her with what was – in the circumstances – a heartbreaking smile.

'You should go, Happy,' said Jo. 'This isn't your fight.'

'But it shouldn't be anyone's fight,' said Happy. 'I don't like fighting. We don't have to fight. I know these lions. They know me. I will talk to them.'

She took a step forward.

One of the cheetahs turned fast at her movement and stopped her in her tracks with a warning snarl.

'Oh!' said Happy, the shock of it jolting a tear from her eye. 'Why—'

As if in answer, the closest lion roared back at the cheetah. The noise echoed around the square, an ancient rumbling sound, and Will felt a lurch in his guts. Happy stumbled back in beside him, behind the dragon shield. This time when she looked up at him and Jo her cheeks were wet and the smile was gone.

'But normally—' she began, her lip quivering.

'Happy, they're not normal,' said Tragedy. 'Look at their eyes.'

All the lions' eyes had the cold blue fire of the ancient magic blazing out of them.

'Bast's got them under her spell,' said Will.

'Don't worry,' said Tragedy, sounding unfeasibly cheery. 'It's only magic. We've got the antidote.'

And he turned and winked at Wolfie.

'Go on then, maestro, time to give it some elbow.'

'Wiz pleasure,' said Wolfie, shaking the frills on his cuff free as he stuck the violin under his chin and flexed his bow.

'What?' said Jo.

'No,' said Will, who had the advantage of having seen Wolfie's music work its charm at calming the savage beasts that had trapped him in Oxford Street earlier. 'No, Jo, just watch. It really works.'

The lurch was gone from his guts and they no longer felt half as watery as they had a moment ago when he'd mistakenly thought that all was lost.

'Just get ready to move while he keeps their attention. It's going to be OK.'

'Yeah,' grinned Tragedy. 'That cat in the museum might have magic, but we've got something better: we've got *arpeggios*!'

'Arpeggi-what?' said Jo.

'Ziss!' said Wolfie, and he took a bold step forward, a wild smile on his face. 'Listen and zee!'

He faced the closest lion and bowed gracefully, violin still tucked under his chin, the free hand with the bow held out in a wide and graceful flourish as he did so.

The lion actually cocked its head to one side in surprise.

''E's *such* a bleedin' show-off,' grinned Tragedy. 'But you can't fault him for it, not when he delivers the goods like he does. He's some musician, no doubt about it.'

Wolfie turned back for an instant

'*Wunderkind*,' he said, eyes sparkling. 'Not a mere musician. A szparkling *wunderkind*!'

And then he turned back and started to play – and two things happened at once.

The first note soared up into the sky, and something dark dive-bombed down out of the same sky and seemed to clip him on the arm.

He stumbled back, the violin suddenly silenced, and stared in shock as the black bomb reversed its abrupt descent and flapped back above the rooftops.

'Vot ze— But – vot . . . ?' Wolfie stuttered, staring

at his bow hand, which was now empty.

They all looked upwards.

The bomb was not a bomb but a bird, and not just any bird but a black stone hawk with a piercing-blue eye and what was undoubtedly Wolfie's violin bow held in its beak.

'But zat's, zat's—'

'That's Horus the bleedin' hawk,' said Tragedy in disgust. 'Bast's bleeedin' eye-in-the-sky.'

They watched the hawk flap off in the general direction of the museum.

'But . . . zat beastly bird has burgled me of my bow!' quivered Wolfie, suddenly not sounding or looking like a *wunderkind* so much as a small boy who'd had a favourite toy snatched away by a bully.

'No. That's Plan A gone for a Burton,' corrected Tragedy.

Will felt the despair lurch back into his guts. Jo gripped his hand and squeezed. He met her eyes and saw her jerk her head towards Farty.

'Lions don't like fire, do they?' she said.

'Normal ones don't,' he said carefully, trying not to extinguish the little spark of hope her words had kindled inside.

'But his fire's not the normal kind either,' she said.

18

'No,' he agreed. 'No, it isn't.'

'Plan B,' she said.

They both looked down at Happy.

'I'll ask,' she said, and turned to speak quietly to the dragon.

The lion to which Wolfie had bowed uncocked its head and dropped low to the ground, its chest grazing the pavement as it began to inch towards them, unmistakably stalking closer for the kill.

The cheetahs growled a warning and lashed their tails slowly back and forth as they faced the tightening ring of lions moving in on all sides.

'Even if he could just sort of clear a path to that house over there, the one with the open door,' said Will, looking around the square, trying to see where the lions were at their thinnest.

A door that was already open would be perfect and save them the potentially fatal inconvenience of running for safety and finding a locked door between them and it.

'Oook,' said the dragon, and stepped to the fore. He seemed to nod at Will and Jo, and then he roared at the lions and took a deep whooshing in-breath. The lions paused and watched as the silver beast rotated his head, looking from one side to the other as the heat in his fire-crop built to orange then to red, then to a white-hot glow in his throat.

The lions all battened back their ears as if on cue and took a couple of hesitant steps back. The dragon stepped forward and pointed at the open door with one stubby claw, looking back at Will as if for confirmation.

Will nodded.

'Get ready to run,' he said.

Guy the Gorilla scooped Happy under his arm.

The lions might have been wary of the dragon but they weren't cowardly. The lion facing it, the one in the line of fire, snarled defiantly back at it.

'NOW!' said Will.

The dragon snapped his head forward like a cobra striking, his eyes hot and angry, his fanged mouth gaping wide to unleash the banked-up wildfire in his fire-crop.

A small and not very impressive burp plopped out towards the lion.

Behind the dragon a much, *much* more impressive whoosh of wildfire smoked a dark streak across the tarmac and ignited a pile of bin bags that had been neatly set out for collection on the pavement.

The dragon whimpered and tried to reach back and

hold his bottom with his inadequately short arms, then saw another puddle and sat quickly down in the water, which immediately turned to steam.

'Oh, Guy,' said Happy, looking up at the gorilla. 'I think you did break this poor dragon.'

The gorilla shrugged apologetically, which, given the whole massive structure of muscle hunched across his shoulders, was quite a substantial show of regret.

'At least we weren't standing right behind it,' said Tragedy. 'Cor, we'd have been toast. Literally.'

'We are toast,' said Jo, voice dull, looking at the cordon of lions now moving in again. 'Unless anyone's got a Plan C?'

The gorilla put Happy down on the back of one of the cheetahs. She buried her hands in its fur and held on. Then Guy turned back and gave Will and Jo a look that was very human: there were no words, other than a deep bass grunt, but he pointed at the open door and then thumped his chest, and as clear as day they understood that he was saying they should all run for it when he made a hole for them.

'I'd say we got us a Plan G,' gulped Tragedy. 'You go for it, big man.'

Guy the Gorilla turned to the lions and reared up on his back legs, suddenly becoming a looming two-metre-tall thundercloud of bunched muscle and pent-up aggression just waiting to explode, and he grunted and barked and smacked his giant pile-driver fists against his chest as he faced down the whole London Pride.

It might have been a last, futile gesture of defiance, outnumbered as he was, but it was undeniably effective.

His mouth opened to reveal four great fangs that were just as brutal as the ones in the lions' mouths, and his eyes seemed to retreat back beneath heavy brows as they lost the human look and became the dark distillation of brute animal power.

He roared again, and thumped his chest in a full three hundred and sixty degrees, barking and feinting at any lion that dared to get a step closer than any of the others. And the more he faced down the lions the angrier they seemed to get, ears back, snarling, tails lashing, matching his barking and roaring with snarls and roars of their own. The ground seemed to shake and rumble under their feet at the intensity of this display of defiance.

'I've never seen him like this,' said Happy, sounding both awestruck and more than a little disturbed. 'He's normally such a big, gentle fellow.'

'He's protecting you,' said Jo.

'I don't want to see him get hurt,' said Happy. 'I don't want to see anyone or any animal get hurt.'

'Yeah, well, Hap, you might have to close your eyes then,' said Tragedy. 'Cos everything's about to kick off.'

And then it did.

A lion made from pale Portland stone leapt at Guy, and the gorilla just stood there like a boxer and punched it with a fist like a steam-hammer.

There was a massive THONK sound of metal hitting rock, and the lion dropped to the ground, out cold. A second lion, made of weather-tarnished bronze, leapt for him but was T-boned by one of the cheetahs, who hit it amidships and held on, so that the two statues collapsed into a whirling tangle of snarling mouths and slashing claws.

A third lion pounced towards Will and Joe, and for an instant Jo thought the world had gone into slow motion – she saw the gaping mouthful of fangs heading right for her head, getting bigger with horrific muscle-freezing speed, and before she could even think about dodging . . .

. . . the mouth stopped dead in mid-air.

It seemed to hang there, inches in front of her face, like cartoon characters do when they run over the edge of a cliff, just before plunging downwards.

Except this lion didn't drop . . .

It jerked backwards with a surprised yelp.

Guy the Gorilla had caught it by the tail and now yanked it backwards. He kept hold of the tail and began to whirl the surprised and outraged lion round his head like a hammer-thrower, or someone whirling a battleaxe.

He advanced on the line of lions between him and the open door, using the whirling lion to clear a path for his friends. They crouched and kept close to him, like people huddling beneath the blades of a helicopter, moving as he did, inch by inch towards safety.

It was a good plan, right up until Guy's lion-club smacked one of the bigger lions on the nose, and it leapt backwards with a shrowl of affronted fury and hunched defensively in the very doorway through which they were hoping to escape.

Will had been inching forward, keeping the dragon shield ready to protect their rear, in case the cheetah that was backing them up should fail to stop any lion who attacked from that direction.

He looked quickly behind them and saw the lions

there were indeed closing in fast. He turned back to warn Jo and was shocked to find she was suddenly tugged out of his field of vision and being jerked violently up into the sky.

# 3

## *Dogfight (with Lions)*

Will lifted his shield and looked wildly up into the sky, terrified at what he might see, at whatever monster might have grabbed his sister in its talons.

He almost shouted with relief when he saw the golden shape of Ariel hovering above him with an outstretched hand, and beyond her Jo being held in the air by another smiling bronze man in a winged helmet.

'Come on, boy!' she said. 'Time to go.'

He reached up without thinking and felt her lift him and then hold him in place with an arm tightly gripped around his waist. He saw another dark statue with wings swoop in under them as Ariel lofted into the sky, and realised it was one of the Victory Angels scooping Wolfie and Tragedy to safety, holding one under each arm as if they were just parcels and not happily laughing bronze boy-statues.

'What about Happy?' he shouted, swivelling round

to try and get a rear view of the battlefield below. He saw the Guy fling the lion-club into the nearest bunch of attackers, sending them flying every which way, like so many lion-shaped skittles. He grabbed Happy, vaulted over them and scaled the façade of the house as easily as if it were a ladder, getting her to the high ground and safety in no time at all.

He put her gently on the flat roof and then looked down and roared in defiance at the London Pride, beating his chest as he did so.

The cheetahs stopped fighting the moment Happy was safe and ran through the cordon of lions like two matched bronze missiles, streaking for home.

'Don't mention it,' said a slightly huffy voice in his ear.

'I'm sorry,' he said. 'I mean, I'm grateful, very grateful. Thank you. You saved us.'

'Yes I did, didn't I?' she said in that rather-too-pleased-with-herself sort of voice that he was coming to recognise as being her default setting. 'I mean, Merc and me over there, and Quad's Victory too, I suppose. We saved you.'

He recognised the large Victory Angel as the one he had seen earlier, the one normally part of the four-horse chariot statue at Hyde Park Corner called the Quadriga, but he didn't recognise the statue holding Jo, who was grinning like a maniac and waving back at him with her stick.

'That's Merc. Or Mercury. Or Hermes. Messenger of the gods, he calls himself, but in truth the closest he gets to Mount Olympus is the top of the Triton Building in Finsbury Square, where he normally is,' she said. 'He's not got half as smart an address as I do at the bank, I must say, but you'd never know it from his attitude.'

Merc had a tin hat on that looked comfortingly similar to the one the Fusilier wore, but his had little wings on it. Unlike the Fusilier, he wore little else other than a pair of sandals that also had a pair of wings. He carried a strange sort of thing in the hand that wasn't holding Jo, something Will at first thought was a tennis racket, but which, as they all flew closer to each other, he realised was a T-shaped stick with two large snakes twined around it.

'Wotcher, Merc,' shouted Tragedy, who was now flying close to Ariel. He grinned across at Will. 'Saved by the bell, eh.'

'I vant my bow,' said a very aggrieved voice from under the other arm of the Victory. 'Zey took my bow and I vant it back!'

'We'll get you another one,' said Tragedy. 'Chin up.'

'I don't vant to chin up and I don't vant anozzer bow. I vant my bow and I vant it now!' cried Wolfie.

'Just be happy for a moment that we're safe from those lions,' said Tragedy. 'Come on, don't take on so. We're safe as houses up here, cos the lions are down there, and lions can't fly!'

'Er . . .' said Jo.

'Er what?' said Tragedy.

'Er, I don't think you should have said that,' said Jo, and pointed.

There are four lions on the Holborn Viaduct, two at each end.

They're metal and they usually sit there with one paw resting regally (as befits the king of the beasts) on a ball that might or might not represent the world.

The only abnormal thing about them – normally – is that they have two things that other lions don't have: wings. But this was, of course, not anything close to a normal day, and at least two of them had left their perches and used those wings to take to the air. They flew fast and silently, and were heading straight for them.

'Look out!' shouted Will, and then he could say no

more because Ariel had gripped him even tighter. The three flying statues dived as one and began to take evasive action, looping low over the rooftops and jinking left and right. Will felt the speed of their passage through the air buffeting the shield strapped to his arm, and then Ariel banked sharply and the sudden change of direction bounced the edge of the shield into his face with a painful bump that made him see stars. When he shook his head clear there was only Merc and Jo in the air next to him, as the Victory had clearly gone right when they'd gone left.

Ariel and Merc halted at roof level and scanned the sky.

'See anything, Golden Girl?' said Ariel.

She shook her head. 'I think we lost them.'

He nodded. 'Me too. They don't stray far from the viaduct, those lions.'

'Where are we going now?' shouted Jo.

Merc turned to point behind him, and though he got his mouth open to reply, a winged lion barrelled up into him from the street below, knocking all the breath – and any chance of speaking – straight out of him.

He spun in the air with the force of the impact, and Will saw that his first instinct was to wrap both his

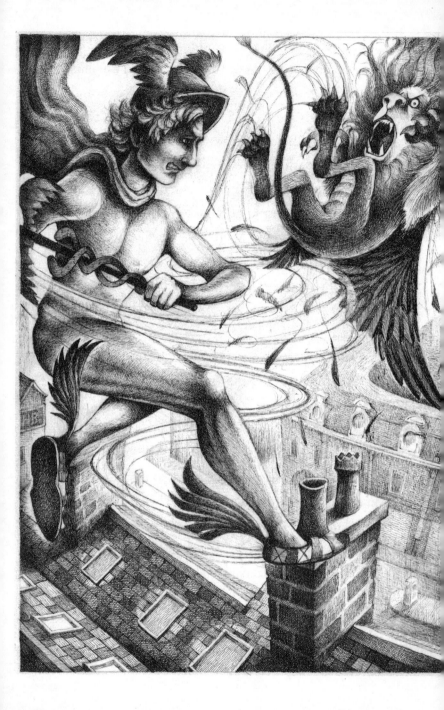

arms round Jo to protect her as they hit the roof.

Merc managed to wrench himself round so that his shoulders took all of the crunching impact, and then as the lion flew back in to attack he managed to swat it with the snake-staff in a backhand volley that was in fact just like a very powerful tennis shot, knocking it senseless and making it drop back to the unseen street below.

'Jo! You OK?' shouted Will.

His heart lifted as she waved back.

'Fine!' she gasped. 'Just winded.'

And then the second winged lion pounced from over the ridge of the roof, and Merc had no time to do anything but instinctively fold himself protectively around her and take the full force of the attack on his already injured back.

The Victory swooped in and – her hands being full of Wolfie and Tragedy – gave the lion a most unladylike but highly effective boot in the ribs that sent it tumbling away. But it just leapt forward again, and Will found with an unpleasant shock that he had wrenched himself free of Ariel's grasp and was falling to the roof three metres below. He heard Ariel's gasp of surprise, and then he hit the pitched slope of the roof, which broke his fall more gently than he'd expected, and slid down to Merc and Jo in a cascade of dislodged slates. He slammed the dragon shield over them and felt the thump of the lion hitting it an instant later.

It took all his own strength and the extra power the shield seemed to give him not to buckle and let the onslaught flatten them all, but he held and pushed back, hurling the yowling lion away a second time.

'Thanks,' grunted Merc. 'Save the girl now. I'm too broken to fight.'

The lion hit them again, slamming into the shield with a metallic thump and a scrabble of claws, but once more Will was able to use the strange power the shield gave him to absorb the shock and protect them, and then push it back off, but not as strongly as before.

'Seriously. Save the girl,' said Merc. 'You don't need to—'

'Yeah I do,' said Will. He was remembering how bad it had been when the Fusilier had been all but destroyed while saving him. 'We'll fight this together.'

He peered round the side of the shield, trying to see when the lion was going to make its third attempt to break through the one-shield wall. It was on the parapet of the building, head lower than its shoulders, muscles bunched to spring, panting slightly. It wasn't the kind of panting that said it was exhausted though.

It was the kind of panting that was more like it was using its tongue to taste the air and get a good scent of its prey,

There was a scrabble on the roof tiles behind him, and he spun, expecting a sneak attack, but it was only Tragedy and Wolfie sliding down into the protected area behind the shield.

'Hoi! Make a hole!' cried Tragedy as he tumbled to a halt at Will's feet. 'Room for two little-uns?'

There wasn't really. Will shrugged and looked back round the edge of the shield. He felt like an oyster waiting to be shucked. The lion was still on the parapet, waiting for its moment.

'Make yourselves useful and brace yourself against the shield,' he ordered through gritted teeth. 'I'll tell you when it moves.'

The lion growled but did not budge.

'Where's the Victory anyway?' said Will. The waiting was killing him.

'Ah,' said Tragedy. 'That would be telling . . .'

The lion suddenly moved but it didn't leap forward. It was yanked backwards by something tugging on its tail, something below the parapet out of sight. It careened backwards, hitting its chin on the parapet, and had just enough time to grab on with its front claws and stop itself being jerked down into the street on top of whatever or whoever had a grip on the end of its tail. It clung there for a moment looking dazed and outraged, and then there was a sudden change of direction and the sound of a mighty pair of wings snapping downwards like a thunderclap. The black bulk of the Quadriga Victory came rocketing up over the parapet as she powered herself straight upwards into the sky, both hands locked on to the lion's tail.

'There she is,' said Tragedy. 'Got the idea from that gorilla, she did.'

They watched her beat her way south across the rooftops, the lion twisting and lashing below her like a very angry pendulum.

'Said she was going to drop it in the Thames,' said Tragedy. 'Hate getting wet, do cats. Teach it a lesson, I reckon.'

Ariel dropped to the roof next to them and pushed her way through to kneel by Merc.

He'd stopped moving and was just staring at the sky, breathing hard, his eyes wide despite the drizzle beginning to spot down on them. Jo rolled out from under his protective embrace.

'How is he?' she said.

'Not good,' said Ariel. 'The fool.'

But she didn't say fool like she meant it. She said it like she rather admired him for his folly.

'I shall have to get him back to his plinth or he'll be stuck like this forever.'

There was the sound of a great commotion in the street below, as if a dustbin lorry full of steam kettles and snarling cats had just careered round the corner. Jo, who was closest to the edge, was first to look over the parapet.

'Will!' she shouted, pointing down. 'The lions are going to get Farty! He doesn't know how to fight backwards.'

It was true. Farty had obviously been trying to follow their progress across the sky by chasing along at street level as best he could. Clearly he had lost the power of flight as well as his dignity when Guy had clamped down on his snout and reversed the natural flow of the wildfire.

He had not been fast enough to escape the London Pride and was surrounded by angry lions who, while still growling with frustration at the escape of their initial prey, were cleverer than the dragon, who clearly didn't have the first idea about how to defend himself with his newly reversed weapon. He would keep trying to spit wildfire at whatever lion was in front of him, but instead incinerate whatever his bottom happened to be pointing at instead.

The lions were keeping well clear of his tail, and though he kept spinning and lashing out at them, each time he fired, the jet of flame was weaker and cooler. The lions were, in fact, just toying with him, like a domestic cat will sometimes just play with a mouse for a long time before administering the final *coup de grâce*.

Will wasn't sure why he felt so sorry or responsible for the confused backward-firing dragon. Maybe it was because he had looked so friendly and grateful at being given a name, even such an unflattering one. Or maybe, probably, in fact most definitely because he kept swatting at the taunting lions with the ragged shards of the plywood GOLF SALE sign.

The GOLF SALE sign that he had equipped himself with to take the place of the shield Will had basically stolen from him.

Will knew, because he could feel the tingle of extra strength the shield seemed to give him, that one of the reasons the beleaguered dragon was in such dire straits was that he was less powerful than he should be, given he was missing an essential part of himself.

Will squirmed round and looked into Ariel's face.

'We've got to save the dragon!'

'You're mad,' she said. 'A, it's a dragon. And B, I can't carry a dragon. I'm not some hulking bruiser with muscles that—'

'Just drop us in low over him,' he said. 'Now! I mean, I wish I could fly and do it myself but I can't and you can, so it's up to you. You can do that, right?'

'I can fly better than anything you ever saw,' she huffed. 'But why should I— Ouch!'

She stared at him in genuine shock.

'Did you just pinch me, boy?'

Will hadn't thought about doing it, it had just happened. But it had got her attention.

'Yes. Sorry. But I'll do it again if you keep on wasting time gabbling and don't get us down there.'

'But why— OUCH!'

'Because he needs protection,' said Will.

Ariel blew out her cheeks in frustration, looking like she was about to say something else, but then clearly decided it would be a waste of breath. She grabbed Will round the waist and dropped off the ledge like a falcon hurtling down at its prey.

And she was right in her assessment of her flying skills, because she came to a precise halt right above the dragon, who was now flailing with increasing weakness at the lions, who were goading him on all sides except the one behind his tail.

'Hey!' shouted Will. The dragon was too busy trying to protect himself from every quarter to look up. Will put his fingers in his mouth and whistled the loud piercing whistle his dad had taught him. Even the lions paused and looked up.

'Hey, Farty! Up here!' shouted Will. 'Behind you!'

The dragon's eyes found him too, and Will was shocked to see they were not only dim with exhaustion, but leaking tears.

Dragons aren't made to cry, and they look disconcertingly vulnerable when they do. Despite that, the dragon sniffed and tried to wave him off, pointing upwards.

'Ook ook ook ook!' it said, urgency in its voice. 'Ook ook ook ook!'

*Get out of here.*

Maybe that's why Will did what he did.

Maybe it was the tears.

Maybe it was the dragon telling him to save himself.

Whatever it was, he shook loose the straps round his arm and tossed down the dragon shield without really thinking about whether this was in fact a very wise thing to do.

He saw Farty's eyes widen in surprise, and then he saw him jump skyward to catch the shield in his scrabbling talons. And then, when he crashed back down on the road, there was a mighty CLANG, as if something much heavier and more dangerous had now landed than the tearful thing that just leapt upwards.

The lions froze.

Farty closed his eyes and grasped the shield tightly, snaking his arm through the straps and settling it comfortably in place. Then he shuddered as a tremble of power coursed through his body.

And then he opened his eyes, and they weren't leaking tears any more. They were red hot and smoking.

And he didn't look *in* trouble any more.

He looked like *the* trouble.

He cricked his neck from side to side, shaking out the stiffness. And then he spat fire. Out of his mouth. The right way. A roiling, twisting rope of wildfire like the jet from a fire hose, a pure standing flame that he arced round himself, creating a wall of protective fire, making the big cats yowl and leap away.

'You mended him,' said Ariel, her voice tinged with wonder.

'It's the shield,' said Will. 'It's part of him, part of

the statue. Taking it was like taking a bit of his brain, a part of his muscles.'

Ariel lofted them back upwards and over the parapet where the others were watching.

Jo clapped Will on the back.

'Good job,' she said.

'Might wish you'd've held onto that shield,' said Tragedy.

Will shrugged. 'He needed it more than me.'

That was true.

But he also knew that what Tragedy had said was true too. He felt strange without the shield. It had definitely given him an extra buzz of power, like a kind of fizz. It had been both a weight to carry and a boost of energy. Up here on the roof, suddenly without it on his arm, he felt a bit shivery and exposed. Maybe it was the drizzle and the light breeze whipping the raindrops into his face. Maybe.

'You OK?' said Jo.

'Yeah,' he said.

'Me neither.' She grinned. Then she lost the momentary smile and looked at Mercury. 'Nor him.'

Merc rolled his head round and his eyes struggled to focus on them.

'Sphinx took a woman to the museum,' he said. 'Was it . . .'

He lost focus for a while and tried to blink the rain out of his eyes.

'Was it your mother?'

'Yes,' said Jo. 'I think so.'

'Sphinx was carrying her carefully,' the broken statue wheezed. 'Cat must want her for something, not want her hurt. Say she's OK for now, I would. Where's your shield . . . you had a shield . . .'

Jo answered. Will let her. He was feeling suddenly very cold and tired.

'He saved a dragon with it. Like you saved me.'

Merc looked hard at Will and didn't speak for a long moment.

'Good man,' he said with a cough. 'Not wise, maybe, but good.' And then he closed his eyes and slumped back on the slates.

'Right,' said Ariel, suddenly sounding as brisk as a nurse and not at all flighty. 'I'm getting him back to his plinth now.'

Merc suddenly jerked his eyes open and his hand grabbed Ariel's arm, dragging her close enough to hear what he could now only whisper urgently into her ear.

'No,' she said.

He hissed more urgently.

'He'll break his neck,' she said. 'And she needs a stick to walk. They'll both break their—'

Merc found enough voice for Jo and Will to hear him insist.

'They need our help. That's all I can give them now. Do it, you infuriating girl.'

And then his eyes rolled back and he was gone. Ariel looked at him and cleared her throat.

'Idiot,' she said.

'Get him to his plinth!' said Will. He knew the only way Merc would revive was if he was on his plinth at midnight. And since anything could happen out of nowhere, if something was to be done it should be done immediately, before that 'anything' turned into a pack of howling dragons or a pride of hungry stone lions.

Ariel didn't pick Merc up right away. Instead she unfastened one of his winged sandals and then the other. Then she carefully unbuckled the chinstrap on the winged helmet and took it off his head. This revealed his face and hair. She paused for a moment and pushed the hair out of his eyes. His face, now they could see it properly, was younger and handsomer than Jo had expected. She saw Ariel's

44

face looking down at it and glanced away.

She could see Ariel liked him a lot, and that it was a secret.

'What?' said Ariel, catching her. Her voice was defensive.

'Nothing,' said Jo.

'No,' said Will, who'd seen the same thing. 'What's going to break our necks?' he asked,

Ariel held out the sandals and the hat.

'These are.'

'What do you mean?' said Will.

'You wished you could fly,' said Tragedy.

'Ja,' said Wolfie. 'No, I *totally* heard you say zat.'

'Too late to be careful what you wish for,' said Ariel. 'You just got it.'

# 4

## Cat and Dog

Between the shock and confusion of discovering that Jo and Will's mother was not where they expected her to be, and the subsequent attack by the waiting dragon, everyone lost track of Filax.

Filax, the great marble Molossian hound, did not, however, lose track of what had got him by the nose. And that was the scent of their mother.

He had smelled the wallet, which was all that was left to show of where she had been taken from, and he had put his nose to the ground and started following the trail. He snaked across the square and down a side street, and as he did so he paid little attention to the lions coming in the other direction. The lions, who were neither looking for dogs nor had any reason to suspect that Filax – like all the other animal statues – was not under the spell of Bast's magic, ignored him right back.

Filax, once on the trail of something, was focused

and almost impossible to distract. He was, in fact, the perfect example of doggedness, from the point of his nose to the tip of his tail.

He wove his way through the frozen people on the pavement and picked up speed as the scent-trail moved out into the centre of the street and followed a straighter line. As he trotted ahead, the invisible ribbon of scent became stronger and fresher.

He knew he was gaining on it. That was good.

What was bad was as the scent became stronger and stronger, he realised that it was interwoven with another aroma. A dog's nose is a highly sophisticated instrument, picking up clues from the merest hint of a smell that lesser noses couldn't even notice: the story told by this closely twined pair of smells wasn't a very welcome one, but this fact did not slow his pursuit. The other smell was not 'mother', but 'cat', or 'almost cat' and something that a normal cat shouldn't smell of.

Cat was, for many reasons, one of the smells that Filax didn't like on a good day, and since Bast had been released, things had gone bad fast, and the epicentre of that blast of malign magic was, of course, a cat.

The cat that he was trailing wasn't Bast, but it did

have an overtone to its smell that was a bit Bast-ish. It was also an overpowering smell, which told Filax's highly developed nose that it was following a giant cat. And the extra thing that a cat shouldn't also smell of, that this particular cat *did* smell of, was human.

There's only one kind of creature among the many and varied statues of London that is both cat and human, of course, and that's precisely what Filax was on the trail of.

The bit of the story that even his highly tuned nose had not been able to tell him was this: when the dragon had come back to the first place it had ever encountered Jo and Will, he had had a plan. And that plan was simple: Will had defeated him and stolen his shield. He was going to steal their mother and give her to Bast, so that Bast would help him get his shield back, maybe swapping one for the other. Doing this was both smart (because the dragon wasn't really so good at thinking for himself and so could have done with some help making a plan like that work) and not so smart (because Bast wasn't interested in helping anyone but Bast).

The dragon had been accompanied to the ambush by one of the giant Sphinxes that normally guarded Cleopatra's Needle on the side of the Thames. It was about the size of an elephant, with the body of a lion and the head of a man wearing an Egyptian headdress. This was the half-man, half-cat and slightly Bast-ish smell that Filax now had in his nostrils.

The Sphinx had had no interest in staying and helping the dragon. It had just waited until he had sheepishly pointed out which of the pathetically frozen pedestrians was the one Jo and Will had been especially interested in, and then it had bent down and neatly taken the back of her coat in its jaws and lifted her into the air just as a smaller cat would carry a mouse, and headed slowly back to the museum.

It moved slowly not just because it felt no urgency, but because it was a Sphinx, and Sphinxes simply do not hurry. They move majestically and enigmatically, and expect other things to move out of their way.

This particular Sphinx was the least human of the two Sphinxes at Cleopatra's Needle, having been damaged in the past by stupid people dropping bombs out of the sky.

It still bore both the small shrapnel holes of that explosion, and a very large grudge against humanity in general.

That was why it was helping Bast. It wanted to see what would happen.

It wasn't bad, especially, but its sense of mischief was coloured by a streak of malice. Mainly it was bored, because sitting beside the Thames and watching the traffic, or being sat on by groups of children wanting to have their picture taken with it wasn't really stimulating.

Filax was head down and moving faster and faster as the scent grew stronger. And because he was really 'seeing' with his nose and not his eyes (and as he caught up with the Sphinx just as it had turned a corner), he very nearly crashed right into it.

'Mind yourself, dog,' said the Sphinx, turning round to look at what the sudden movement in the otherwise motionless street was. It sounded bored and mildly offended. 'I am walking here.'

Filax saw the children's mother dangling awkwardly from the Sphinx's mouth, lifeless as a doll, a long strand of aubergine-dark hair swinging free of the hat she was wearing. She looked like Jo, and she smelled like her and Will.

It occurred to Filax as he watched the head turn away and the Sphinx prowl onwards towards the museum across the street that he had a choice: he could go back to the children and tell them where their mother was, through the girl Happy, who could understand what animals said, or he could try and rescue her himself.

Of course, the second choice would mean following the Sphinx into the doors of the museum, doors that were even now opening like a dark mouth to allow it in.

The museum was Filax's home. It was also full of cat-headed statues that had delighted in tormenting and hurting him the moment Bast's release back into the world had given them power to do so. As far as he knew they had done it simply because they were cats and he was a dog. The museum was a home that had become a place of pain and danger for him, a home he had escaped from. It was a place only a fool would go back to.

A fool or a hero.

Filax was not a fool. He was a dog.

And in his mind, and in his great heart, that meant the hero part came as standard.

He trotted forward and sneaked into the museum right on the tail of the Sphinx, just before the massive doors slammed shut behind them.

# 5

## *Everyone Wants to Fly*

Everyone wants to fly.

Nobody wants to fall.

That was the thought going through Will's head as he looked down at the winged sandals and the helmet.

'You think there's a trick to it?' he said.

'Probably,' said Jo. 'My guess is the trick is not dropping out of the sky and plunging to a horrible painful death.'

'Oh good,' he said. 'And there was me thinking there would be more to it than that.' He poked the helmet with his foot. 'That sounds easy.'

Jo laughed hollowly. 'Yep,' she said. 'Or we could just walk.'

'Thing is,' said Will, 'and I'm just saying, for the sake of argument, I've always— What are you doing?'

Jo had moved past him and was sitting down on the roof.

'I'm bagging the sandals before you do,' she said.

'It's not like we're *not* going to try, is it? Because I know we could spend lots of time worrying about it and talking round and round, but in the end I also know we both think being able to fly would be the second-coolest thing in the world, right?'

She looked very smug, somehow. And the fact she was correct made it all the more annoying.

'What's the coolest thing then?' he said.

She stopped lacing the sandals on over her boots and tossed him the helmet.

'Rescuing Mum, of course, doofus.'

He looked at the helmet. It was heavy and, now he was examining it close to, he could see that it was exactly like the ones the statues of the World War One Tommies all wore, except it had a pair of small wings folded neatly on either side.

He watched his sister cinch the sandals tight like a pair of over-boots. She caught his eye and stopped.

'What?'

'How come I get the helmet?'

'Cos you snoozed . . . and you losed, bro,' she said, reaching out a hand. He pulled her to her feet. 'Whoa!' Her legs bobbled beneath her a little bit. He held her steady. 'OK,' she said. 'I'm OK.'

'Sure?' he asked. He knew falling over was worse

for her than him on account of her knee injury.

'Yeah. A bit like being on roller skates.' She gingerly let go and checked her balance. 'Yeah. Really slippery roller skates that want to go in all directions, sideways as well as forwards and backwards . . . but kind of cool too.'

She smiled and walked a few steps, keeping her hand on the waist-high wall of the parapet, then turned and walked back to him.

'Go on then,' she said. 'Put it on.'

He looked at the helmet, grimaced a little, and lifted it up and on top of his head.

'Wow!' he said. 'It really is heavy.'

'And pleasingly dorky,' she grinned. 'You look a real durr in it. Knew you would. That's why I grabbed the natty footwear.'

'Do up the chinstrap,' said Tragedy. 'Got to buckle in, you do. Important safety feature.'

He found the buckle on the strap and cinched it tight. He gulped.

'You don't have to have it so snug,' said Tragedy. 'You'll cut off all the blood to your brain and then where'll you be?'

'Totally off your noodle,' said Tragedy. 'Zat's where you'll be.'

'Right,' said Will, loosening the strap and raising an eyebrow at his sister.

'Don't worry about that,' said Jo. 'He hasn't been on his noodle for years.'

'What's a noodle?' whispered Will.

'No idea,' she said. 'But Wolfie's— What?'

Will was staring at her in shock. Eye to eye. Literally.

'You're taller than me,' he said. 'I mean, you're shorter than me, but now you're the same— Oh!'

He looked down.

'Yeah,' she said. And then she laughed. 'Oh yeah. Totally cool, right?'

Her feet were off the ground. The wings on the sides of the sandals were whirring like hummingbirds, a blur of motion, and she was unmistakably airborne.

'You're flying,' he said. 'How did you . . . ?'

'I just kind of *thought* it,' she said. 'I thought I wanted to fly and then— Wow, watch it!'

She stumbled backwards, hands flailing to stop herself falling.

Will had thought about flying and had suddenly zoomed straight up like a rocket.

He had just time to think he didn't want to be so high and wanted to have his feet on solid ground when he was plummeting back down towards the roof. He saw Tragedy, Wolfie and Jo throw themselves in three different directions to avoid him landing on them, and then he scrunched his eye reflexively shut and braced himself for a painful landing.

And then he stopped.

Abruptly.

But softly, as if he hadn't been moving at all. As if he'd just stepped onto a feather bed. He opened his eyes.

'OK,' he grinned. 'That is seriously awesome.'

Jo was lying sprawled on the roof tiles. She picked up her stick and pushed back up on to her feet.

'Just give us some warning if you're going to do that again,' she said.

And then she flew straight up into the air, higher and higher, and started twisting, corkscrewing round and getting smaller and smaller as she climbed towards the cloud base pushing in above them. And then, just as Will felt a great lurch of worry that all this was going to end in tears, she swooped back down towards them in a long curving loop, still twirling like an ice-skater, sending the raindrops flying off her with the centrifugal force so that it looked like she was spinning her own silvery tutu.

And as she came closer he heard her laughter: wild, open-throated laughter that sounded like pure unfettered joy. And Will found himself joining in the laughter because it was not only highly infectious, but was a sound he had not heard coming from her lips since she fell off the roof and broke her leg a long time ago.

It was the sound of the old Jo, the real one he hadn't even realised he had been missing for so long.

She looped in and tried to spot a landing along the ridge of the roof above them, but her incoming velocity sent her into a long slide that kicked up a wall of spray and sent her towards the steep drop-off at the gable end.

'Jo! Watch—' shouted Will, but before he could finish the warning she'd calmly reached out with her walking stick and hooked it round the pole of a TV aerial, swinging it right round in a full one-eighty. She hung there, panting and laughing.

'You're a nutter,' he said.

'Maybe,' she said, wiping her eyes and getting herself together. 'But you know the really great thing about it?'

'That you didn't plunge out of the sky to a horrible death?' he said.

'That when I'm flying my knee doesn't hurt at all.'

He returned her smile.

'That is great.'

'Well, come on then,' said Tragedy. 'Merc didn't just give you his toys for fun, y'know. He gave us a message to deliver. We got to get over to St Pancras and tell the Betch there's a Bridge Moot.'

'A what?' said Jo.

'Meeting of all the statues, on Tower Bridge.'

'On a bridge?' said Jo. 'Why?'

'Over running water, see, to protect from any bad magic going round. Old tradition it is, works like a charm. Is a charm, I suppose, come to think of it.'

'OK,' said Will. 'But—'

'No buts,' said Wolfie. 'Zis is not "but" time. Zis is "Fetch the Betch" time. We go now!'

'Fine,' said Will. 'But what I was going to say was how are you going to get there?'

'Yes,' said Jo. 'How will you keep up? We can go pretty fast now.'

'Oh, we won't have to keep up,' said Tragedy. 'We're coming with you, ain't we.'

'But how?' said Will. 'You can't fly.'

'No,' said Wolfie. 'Zis is actual fact. But iz not a problem. We do zee piggyback.'

'Yeah,' said Tragedy. 'Piggybacks, see?'

'But—' said Jo.

'I told you,' said Wolfie, waving a finger at her. 'Iz not "but" time. Don't vorry. Iz easy.'

'We do it all the time,' agreed Tragedy. 'Just like riding a bike.'

'Yeah,' said Will about three minutes later, as he swerved round a tower block, wobbling dangerously in the air as he did so. 'Just like riding a bike is fine for you, not so great for the bike . . .'

Flying was mind-blowingly wild and great, but having a bronze violinist clamped to his back like a heavy satchel who shouted directions in his ear all the time was distinctly putting a crimp in the wonderment. Especially because Wolfie kept twisting and turning to point at things in the frozen streets below, or yelling at Tragedy, who was clamped round Jo's back a few metres to their right.

His moving about kept throwing Will's balance off centre and he had a real fear that if he kept on doing it, it wouldn't be long until he capsized in mid-air. And he didn't have full confidence that the winged hat worked upside down.

'Look, stop moving around,' he said. 'You're jerking about like you've got ants in your pants.'

'Zer are no ants,' said Wolfie, sounding offended. 'No ants in zee pants. I am a very good passenger. I do zis all zee time . . .'

'Well, I don't,' said Will. 'So do me a favour and keep still.'

Wolfie harrumphed, but stopped moving.

Will was able to enjoy the sensation much better now.

The helmet had a strange effect that made him feel light-headed. It was as if the normal pull of gravity on his feet was somehow being reversed by a counter-pull from the helmet itself, as if the hat was making him weightless and the whirring wings were doing all the propelling forwards and back. He wanted to laugh like Jo had, but he clenched his teeth and thought of his mother.

The flying was a joy, but there were darker things afoot that would very likely stamp all over this brief moment of fun, and do so all the faster if he let himself give in to the exhilaration.

'Cheer up,' said a voice in his ear. He looked round and jerked in surprise to see Jo's face right next to his, but, even more disconcertingly, upside down. Trust her to try the upside-down thing to see if it worked.

'Steady,' yelped Wolfie, gripping all the tighter.

'No ants in zee pants from you now!'

'Hang on!' shouted Tragedy, pointing ahead. 'Something's up with St Pancras. Slow down a minute!'

Jo and Will came to a halt in mid-air. There was a moment of ungainliness as she slowly tumbled herself right way up and pushed the hair out of her eyes, and then they both let their gaze follow the direction of Tragedy's outstretched arm.

The unmistakable gothic façade of St Pancras station was right ahead of them like a great orange cathedral, and from this height, higher than the clock tower at the western end of the building, they could see beyond the ornate red-brick cliff facing the street, and make out the long steel and glass curve of the train-shed roof beyond.

Beneath the glass something was moving, something that strobed and shuddered and caught the eye like a hook. It was a solid ray of blue light that lanced out of the end of the train shed like a thick laser beam, pointing north.

'What is it?' said Will quietly.

The light was chopping and jumping, as if someone was wrestling with it.

'Dunno,' said Tragedy. 'It's either something bad or something good.'

'Helpful,' said Jo in a tone that made it clear it wasn't.

'I mean, blue light, that's time magic,' said Tragedy. 'That's what's got everything frozen and banged up, isn't it!'

'I don't know,' said Will.

'Well, it is,' said Tragedy. 'Everyone knows that.'

'But it's moving,' said Jo. 'We've seen everyone who's frozen stuck in the blue light, but—'

'But it might not be the sztinking cat,' said Wolfie excitedly. 'It might be something else!'

'Like what?' said Will.

'There's a big old clock face under there,' said Tragedy. 'I mean big, like a real stonker. It's about where that light seems to be beaming out of.'

'So . . . ?' said Jo.

'So maybe it's the cat's magic, or perhaps it's someone trying to wrestle with it,' said Tragedy. 'Maybe it's someone trying to put time back in joint.'

'A statue?' said Will.

'No,' said Wolfie. 'Not a statue.'

'A person? Like us?' said Will.

'No,' said Wolfie with an emphatic shake of his head. 'At least, not any more. Not a person like you at all.'

'They don't know,' said Tragedy.

'Don't know what?' said Will and Jo at the same time.

'Don't know there's not just people and statues. There's the others,' said Tragedy.

'Others?' said Will, looking at Jo. She shrugged.

'The weirded,' said Tragedy.

'Who are the weirded?' said Jo.

'Them vot is cursed,' said Wolfie. 'Cursed to live in zee layer of London that normal people cannot see.'

'Cursed?' said Will. Cursed didn't sound good at all. 'Why cursed?'

'Well. Not polite to ask,' said Tragedy. 'But I reckon that might be the Clocker trying to put time back in joint. He's OK is Old Clocker. Come on, let's go see—'

'Wait!' said Jo. 'Weirded, cursed . . . What if it isn't him?'

'Dunno,' said Tragedy. 'But we got to go under there anyway cos that's where we'll find Betch. Just keep your eyes peeled and be ready to scarper toot sweet if I say so.'

# 6

## *Malice Unchains*

Filax was able to walk into the museum without any of the animal statues thronging the steps or the great covered courtyard within taking any notice of him whatsoever. Even the two cat-headed warriors guarding the doors missed him. All the eyes were on the giant Sphinx and the human prey it was carrying. The Sphinx moved with a calm majesty that pulled the eye towards it, as if it was leading a stately procession of one. The sense that it was important crackled about it like static. As the guards slammed the museum doors behind it, Filax made sure none of the other cat-headed warriors who were Bast's bodyguards (and his ancient tormentors) spotted him, but he kept as close to the Sphinx as he could.

As he sloped between the legs of larger beasts, he noted the unfamiliar dome of wildfire that imprisoned the Temple Bar dragon, but he had little time to pay much attention as he didn't want to lose sight of Jo and Will's mother.

The crowd of animals parted and made a space that led into the Egyptian Gallery. The Sphinx walked through the great doors into a space lit with the flickering blue light that rippled out from the black stone sarcophagus that was the source of Bast's power. The cat was standing on the back of the giant stone scarab nearby, like a general on a tank.

The cat-headed guards stood around her in a half-circle.

Filax slipped through the doors and found a place in the shadows from which to watch unseen.

WHAT IS THIS? hissed Bast as the Sphinx approached.

'What it appears to be,' said the Sphinx, daintily putting the children's mother on the ground with such precision that she stayed on her feet, her face as blank and unmoving as a waxwork. 'A woman. A mother. The children's mother. Nothing special.'

AND YET THE CHILDREN ARE SPECIAL, said Bast, hopping off the back of the scarab and circling in a figure of eight around the woman's legs, rubbing herself against them and smelling her with a wrinkle of the nose that made the nose ring flash in the blue light spilling from the band of hieroglyphs

66

that circled the outside edge of the sarcophagus.

The Sphinx eyed the sarcophagus with a calm and seemingly disinterested eye. It took in the tableau of white-coated staff frozen in the act of replacing the broken fragment that completed the flow of hieroglyphs.

'They mended the inscription,' it said.

YES, said Bast with a hiss of satisfaction. THEY UNBOUND ME.

'Foolish of them,' said the Sphinx. 'Lucky for you.'

Bast shuddered as if luck was something distasteful.

THAT IS OF NO MATTER. WHAT MATTERS IS THIS: WHY ARE THE CHILDREN SPECIAL?

'Why are you asking me?' said the Sphinx.

Bast stopped and looked up at the human face staring back down at her.

YOU DO NOT ASK ME QUESTIONS! I AM BAST.

'And I am a great Sphinx,' said the Sphinx. 'You do not command me. I am an ally. Not a subject.'

I COULD MAKE YOU A SUBJECT, said Bast, a purr of threat rumbling through her voice. She looked at the door to the Great Hall where the Temple Bar dragon was still trapped in the cage of flame Bast had imprisoned him in.

'I am not a lizard,' said the Sphinx contemptuously. 'The same power that flows in you flows in me, though in a different way. I cannot do what you do, but you cannot do to me what you do to others. I am immune.'

YOU LIE.

'I do not lie,' said the Sphinx. 'I don't have to. The only way to control me is to answer one of my riddles. You know this. I am a Sphinx. Neither human nor animal; neither man nor god. Something in between. I cannot take action against you, nor am I meant to harm men for no reason. I am an autonomy and an enigma.'

LONG WORDS DO NOT INTEREST ME.

Bast hissed and stalked away, then walked back, her face as close to a scowl as a cat could get.

IF I ANSWER YOUR RIDDLE WILL YOU TELL ME WHY THE CHILDREN ARE SPECIAL?

'No,' sighed the Sphinx. 'Because I do not know.'

WHO DOES?

'They do, I imagine,' replied the Sphinx. 'You could ask them if you catch them.'

IF I CATCH THEM I SHALL KILL THEM.

Filax growled quietly in the shadows, and then remembered he was meant to be hiding, and stopped before anything noticed him. But the hair on his hackles bristled like a hedgehog, and his mouth curled in a silent snarl.

The Sphinx peered at the cat with genuine interest, forgetting to look bored.

'You would kill them?'

YES.

'Really kill them?'

YES . . . EVENTUALLY.

Bast smirked. A cat smirking is not an attractive sight.

The Sphinx, on the other hand, remained entirely expressionless.

Only another Sphinx would have been able to see that behind the unfathomable mask its mind was whirring with the implications of what the cat had said.

'Well then, I think I hope you don't catch them,' said the Sphinx eventually.

Bast turned and hissed at it in outrage

BUT THEY HAVE DEFIED ME. I AM THE MIGHTY BAST!

Only the fact that the Sphinx's tail made a slow and sinuous shape betrayed its feelings. Its face and voice remained calm.

'You don't have to kill them. And if you want to know why they are special, why not just ask her?' She looked at the children's mother. 'You froze her.'

YES.

'Unfreeze her, then maybe you could ask. She would know, wouldn't she? Mothers know about their children.'

Bast cocked her head on one side, as if thinking.

Then she leapt up onto the rim of the sarcophagus, dabbed a paw into the pool of blue light within and flicked it at the frozen woman.

MOVE FREE. UNBIND EYES. LOOSEN TONGUE!

Bast's voice echoed round the cavernous room like a thunderclap. The woman twitched. Then shivered. Then sneezed three times.

Then she looked around with astonishment.

'Oh!' she said, eyes so wide she seemed to take everything in at once. 'Oh no . . .'

Bast leapt on top of the plinth in front of her.

The Sphinx hissed.

'Stop! She cannot see you! If she could see you, you would have to harm her again, for she would be a thing of power and might try to help her children! But she is harmless. She is nothing.'

The mother's eyes seemed to change a little. Almost as if she had heard the warning in the Sphinx's voice.

But it might have been a trick of the light.

Bast leaned forward and looked deep into her eyes.

I AM BAST THE MIGHTY. WHAT IS THE POWER YOUR CHILDREN WIELD THAT CAN RESIST MY CURSE?

The woman stared straight through the cat as if she wasn't there.

'Why isn't anyone moving?' she said in wonder. 'Is this a nightmare?'

'See? She thinks she's dreaming,' said the Sphinx sharply. 'She can't see you.'

OF COURSE SHE CAN SEE ME, said Bast. I AM MIGHTY—

'Yes,' interrupted the Sphinx, speaking deliberately, almost as if it was speaking to someone other than the cat alone. 'You are Mighty Bast and you have been freed to work your revenge on mankind because those poor fools in the white coats over there made the mistake of mending the ancient curse by replacing the broken bit of stone on the sarcophagus. You've told me all of that, but that's not the point . . .'

Bast hopped up and down in frustration, earrings jiggling.

BUT I LIFTED MY SPELL! SHE CAN MOVE AND SEE LIKE ALL— OH.

Bast sat back on her haunches.

SHE CAN SEE LIKE ALL PEOPLE CAN NORMALLY SEE. WHICH IS NOT ENOUGH TO SEE US, YES?

Bast's voice dripped disappointment.

'Ah. Yes,' said the Sphinx. 'Yes. I am sorry. You are mightier than me in the thinking department, Oh, Bast. I had not thought of that. She can only see like a normal person, and normal people do not see statues move, do they? They cannot see into this layer of the world. Their minds do not let them see the deeper levels of unLondon.'

Bast stared at the kids' mother. Her eyes were now definitely unfocused and she was walking as if in a dream, her face a mask of dulled wonder, her fingers trailing over the surfaces of things as she took it all in, She could clearly see the frozen people, because she spoke to them.

'Hello!' she said. 'Hello, excuse me?'

No one moved.

'Is this a joke?' she said. 'I think I've had an accident . . . I can't remember why I'm—'

She lurched towards the unmoving group of museum staff in their white coats, hunched around the sarcophagus.

'Hey, are you doctors, is this a prank, am I having an episode . . . ?'

Her fingers reached for the white coat closest to her, which was the one who was holding the fragment in place.

'Excuse m—'

STOP!

The mother froze. Bast stared at her.

'What?' said the Sphinx.

I HAVE SEEN ENOUGH.

'Maybe,' said the Sphinx with a shrug. 'You sounded a bit worried, that's all.'

I NEVER WORRY. I AM BAST. PEOPLE WORRY ABOUT *ME*!

'Well, I'm sure you're right,' said the Sphinx. 'Maybe urgent rather than panicked.'

SHE WAS GETTING TOO CLOSE TO THE INSCRIPTION.

'Ah,' said the Sphinx. 'Well, you wouldn't want her unmending that by mistake, would you? I can see that. What are you going to do with her now?'

SHE CAN'T SEE ME. SO SHE CAN'T ANSWER MY QUESTION. SHE'S USELESS.

'Right. Shall I take her away then?' said the Sphinx, stepping forward.

NO.

Bast stared at the woman in disgust.

THE CHILDREN STILL WANT HER. SHE CAN BE BAIT.

The Sphinx's tail lashed a couple of times. Then it gave a very human shrug and turned away.

'Very well. I will leave you to your games.'

THEY ARE NOT GAMES. THEY ARE REVENGE!

'Whatever they are, I find you . . . bore me with your petty malice,' said the Sphinx, walking out.

It ignored the outraged hiss that followed it. But it did look into the shadows where it, and only it, had heard a dog growl.

There was no dog.

Filax was running. The front doors of the museum were closed and guarded by the cat-headed warriors, but there were other ways in and out of the place, and the building was, after all, his home. He knew his way through the endless warren of tunnels and storage bunkers that lay beneath the public galleries, and right now he was heading for one of the back doors as fast as he could run.

Jo and Will were somewhere out there, and they

needed to know what peril awaited them and their mother if they put a foot wrong.

# 7

## An Eye on the Time

If you want to stay hidden in a landscape, one of the best things you can do is keep still. The hunter's eye will pick up movement even before it picks out a shape or a colour that doesn't match the terrain.

Flying over a still city with two cheerful child-statues riding piggyback might be novel and, in its way, fun.

But it's not inconspicuous.

Will and Jo lofted over the steeply pitched roof of the St Pancras Hotel, keeping low enough to fly between the ornate chimney stacks and gargoyles, one of which Jo was almost sure she saw turning its head to look at them as they passed. Before she could be quite sure, the busy decorative splendour of gothic red brick and stone on the front façade had given way to the dark slate roof studded with blue-painted gable windows, which, in turn, as the chimney stacks flew past on the jumbled ridgeline, revealed the huge calm expanse of metal and glass hidden beyond it.

The great length of the original train shed stretched northwards for more than two hundred metres, its ridgeline at ninety degrees to that of the hotel. Where the hotel roof had been an abrupt watershed, the glass surface of the shed was a very slightly pointed arch, dropping in a generous curve on either side, a long hummock like a drum on its side, rather than a sharp edge. Beyond the original roof was a lower, flat glass roof, a square about two thirds as long, and it was out of the end of this that the blue ray was flickering.

Jo couldn't help but gasp in what was half surprise at the mass of glass, and half pleasure.

'Great, innit?' said Tragedy. 'Old Barlow's Train Shed, that is. Was once the widest and biggest space ever got a roof over it.'

'I've been inside,' said Jo, her eye watching the sparkling glass flow past beneath them, 'but I never saw it from this angle.'

'Flying's the thing,' said Tragedy. 'Gives you a whole new prospec, perspy . . . angle on looking at stuff.'

'Perspective,' said Jo, following Will, who was looping downwards towards the end of the flat roof, where he had decided to go in and see what the light was coming from.

'That as well,' said Tragedy. 'Now, stay close to your brother. We don't want to get split up again.'

It wasn't just the ray of blue light that was sticking out of the end of the train shed – there were two trains frozen in the act of entering (or maybe leaving). They looked like great grey flat-headed snakes, the yellow paint on their driving cabs giving them a strangely reptilian look.

Jo cut an aerial U-turn to fly in under the lip of the roof.

The platforms were thronged with busy commuters now hurriedly going nowhere, a slight blue frost covering them and sparkling a little in the reflected light of the beam. The pale stone floors on which they stood were shiny too, and as they flew across, Jo and Will saw themselves reflected in them.

They didn't see the small dot moving in the other direction, because it was far above them on the other side of the glass roof.

But it saw them.

It was the hunter.

They, by moving, had made themselves the prey.

They skimmed low along the platforms at the end of the station, with the flat roof quite close in above them, and then suddenly they were beneath the much

78

higher vaulted span of the Barlow train shed itself. Abruptly, they felt as if they'd entered a vast, airy cathedral. The spans of pale-blue painted iron and panels of glass soared above them, lifting their spirits. Jo found herself grinning as they sped along the platform beside the long metal worm of a parked-up train, flickering over the longest bar either of them had ever seen, crammed with happy-looking travellers now possibly frozen forever with their laughter and champagne glasses.

Then the glasses caught the flicker of light, and Jo and Will looked up at the same time to see the source of the blue beam.

At the end of the shed, where it met the back of the hotel, there was a flat wall of blue-painted girders arranged in a grid, with glass panes hanging in front of the actual brick wall of the building. At the centre of this massive blanked-off arch was a huge clock face, and it was from this dial that the blue light was shooting, like the horizontal beam of a giant searchlight.

'Wow!' said Jo, coming to a halt an instant before Will. He dropped slowly to the platform and looked up, taking off his helmet to do so. She landed next to him and followed the direction of his eyes.

Wolfie and Tragedy leapt off their backs and ran

forward waving and whistling.

What (or perhaps who) they were whistling at was who (or perhaps what) was making the blue beam flicker: it was difficult to tell whether it was a who or a what, as the intensity of the light made it hard to see exactly what was going on. It was like looking into a very bright torchbeam, but what they seemed to be looking at was a huge statue of a man in a suit holding a smaller, life-sized person in front of the clock face. The smaller figure was windmilling his (or possibly its) arms wildly around, as it tried to do something mysterious, but clearly important, to the hands of the clock. The hands were, of course, not moving, but the figure flailing around yanking on them was more than making up for it with the intensity of his actions. As he moved he was accompanied by a wild jingling noise, a little like sleigh-bells.

What made this even stranger was that there was a second giant statue: a woman leaning against the back wall, apparently entirely uninterested in whatever was going on with the clock face. She had her head down and seemed to be looking into a pocket mirror while she applied lipstick.

Will looked at Jo.

'No idea,' she said.

'That giant man must be Betch,' he said. 'He might not be a soldier, but you can see he'd be able to beat any of the other statues Bast might send to fight. He's huge.'

'Who's she then?' said Jo, nodding at the huge girl, who was now rummaging in her handbag for what turned out to be the biggest hairbrush either of them had ever seen. They watched her start to style her long hair, still completely oblivious to them or the activity going on beside her.

'Mrs Betch?' ventured Jo.

A high-pitched whistle cut through everything. Tragedy was standing at the giant statue's feet, two fingers in his mouth. Wolfie was jumping up and down waving.

'Clocker!' he piped 'Hey zere, Clocker! It's us.'

The figure in the hand of the giant statue turned and looked down. The giant turned and slowly lowered him to the platform level, just as easily as if he was on the arm of a cherry-picker.

Once he was out of the direct beam of the clock face they were able to see he was not a moving statue at all. He was something much stranger.

'Wotcher, Clock,' said Tragedy. 'What you up to?'

'Time,' said the strange figure. 'Am up to time.

As always. Except time not now as always.' He grimaced and pointed jerkily at the clock. 'Time out of joint. Am trying to put it back in.'

He looked at Jo and Will. 'Ah. New friends. Not statues. Normal – but moving. Interesting.'

He leaned forward to peer at them, bending at the waist to get a closer look.

He was certainly the oddest person they had ever seen. His face was thin and careworn, with a long and challenging nose on which he wore a fiercely complicated pair of jeweller's spectacles that had several different magnifying lenses attached to them with cunningly hinged arms, ready to be swung down over the main lenses, lenses that were not clear, but a dark-blue glass. This made him look like two things at once; a blind man, and someone who could see the fine details of anything if he wanted to. His long hair was pulled back from his high forehead and tied with a frayed purple ribbon. It was hard to see if it was actually grey, or just powdered with dust, like the rest of him.

He jingled as he moved his head from one side to the other, taking them in. The noise came from the collection of small metal objects that he wore pinned to the front of the old-fashioned cutaway tailcoat that was buttoned around his lanky, spare frame. The coat was ancient and much-mended, and though it had probably originally been black, it had now become so faded with age that it had turned a kind of dark and dusty green. In fact it was so darned and overstitched with repairs that it was hard to see where the original coat stopped and the neatly applied patches began. The jingling collection of metal objects were attached to the coat with ancient ribbons, or chains, or lengths of waxed string; they were, on closer inspection, all watchmaker's things – tools and winding keys, pocket watches and tiny oil cans, more magnifying glasses and a bewildering selection of springs and screwdrivers in all shapes and sizes.

'You look like a Christmas tree,' said Jo, and immediately realised A) she'd said it out loud, and B) that it had been rude to do so.

If he was offended, the strange man gave no indication. Instead his tight face relaxed into a smile, as he took off his glasses with the air of a man doffing his cap and gave her a very polite bow.

His face, when he straightened up, was somehow younger than she'd expected, and the one eye he regarded them with was a kind one.

'Christmas tree. Yes indeed. Positively festooned.

Tools of the trade. Everything to hand. Save time rummaging. No time to waste. Am Clocker, you see. Delighted to make acquaintance, et cetera . . .'

'I'm Jo,' she said, finding herself wanting to return his bow. She didn't, because it felt like it might be weirdly as if she was mimicking him. Instead she nodded to Will. 'This is Will. My brother.'

'Will. Jo. Good names. Solid. Need to be solid. All this to-do, d'you see?' He tutted and waved a hand airily at the clock above them.

'Time's out of joint,' said a voice behind them.

They spun to see another statue standing behind them. He was, in many ways, the opposite of the Clocker – rounded and short where the Clocker was long and angular; homely and everyday where the Clocker was disconcertingly eccentric in his dress and jerky manner. He wore a flapping raincoat and a pork-pie hat pushed back to reveal a cheery middle-aged face. His trousers strained over a small pot belly and were a little too short for him, revealing more of his ankles than was strictly elegant. He carried a battered bag in one hand and looked, all in all, like a rather untidy schoolmaster from a bygone age.

He raised his hat to them and winked at the jingling man.

'And it's his job to keep an eye on the time, eh, Clocker?'

'And time on my eye,' said the Clocker.

'What?' said Jo.

'Show 'em!' said Tragedy. 'Go on!'

Behind him, the giant statue of the man in the suit who had been carrying him turned back to the matching giant statue of the young woman, who was combing her hair with a kind of pouty look on her face. Jo scarcely registered them, because the Clocker leaned closer to her and Will and pointed at his closed eye.

'Don't be scared. Just looks odd. Doesn't hurt me a bit.'

He opened the eye. It certainly did not look at all like the other one. It wasn't an eyeball at all. It was a watch face. It was faintly blue – like the clock above them – but it pulsed red, as if mirroring the beat of his heart.

'Wow,' said Will. 'Cool.'

Jo thought it was faintly scary

'Not the word I would have chosen,' said the statue in the pork-pie hat. 'It's a mark of his curse, you see, binding him to his job.'

'Oh,' said Will. 'I didn't . . .'

'No matter,' said the Clocker. 'No offence either. Just what it is. But time my job. But time stopped. So. Am endeavouring to mend.'

He waved at the clock on the wall.

'No luck. Betch and I about to go to Bridge Moot. See what's what.'

He nodded towards the shabby statue in the flapping raincoat

'Wait . . . You're Betch?' said Will.

'It appears so,' he replied. 'You seem surprised . . .'

'No,' said Jo, pointing at the giant man, who was whispering into the ear of the giant woman, turning her pout into a smile.

'We just sort of thought *he* was.'

'Him?' said Betch. 'Oh, no. He's a, you know, he's . . .'

'What?' said Will.

'He's, well, they both are really, he's um . . . very . . . involved. With her.'

'And vicey-versa,' said the Clocker.

'Quite a coup to get him to stop the endless canoodling long enough to help the Clocker out, in fact,' said Betch. He lowered his voice. 'They're not too bright, either of them, you see, and the poor sculptor who made them wasn't very good at putting anything else into the statue except their fascination with each other. There, see – they're at it again.'

And they were indeed, two giant figures twined into a passionate embrace.

'Yuck,' said Will.

'Well, yes, possibly,' said Betch. 'Public displays of affection are not everyone's cup of tea, at any rate. And that is certainly the largest one in London and quite out of keeping with the wonderful building all around us, but that's just my little bugbear. Tell me your part in all this shenanigans we seem to be stuck in: I'm sure that's a much bigger and more important thing.'

Jo and Will sat on a bench, and Betch sat next to them, and maybe because they were talking to someone who was so obviously normal and of their time – who was not a soldier or an angel or someone who'd been so important in the past that people had made statues of them – or maybe just because his eyes were kind and he had an encouraging smile, they found themselves pouring out the whole story of what had happened to them. And he nodded and didn't interrupt and was so good at listening that they almost quite forgot that he was made of bronze and wasn't a real person like they were.

When they had finished he looked at the Clocker and said, 'Well, this is a fine old pickle.'

And the Clocker nodded. 'A pickle indeed.'

'Do you mind me asking you a question?' said Jo.

'No,' said Betch. 'Of course not.'

'What are you?'

'I'm just me,' he said. 'Same as you, really.'

'You're obviously someone important, because you've been made into a statue, and Tragedy over there said you'd have an idea what to do,' said Will, looking over at the bench on the other side of the concourse where Tragedy and Wolfie were sitting.

'I'm a poet,' said Betch. 'Nothing special. And I love old buildings like this one. So they put me here.'

Will looked over at Tragedy.

'But why'd he say you would—'

And then something swooped in from behind them in a blur of stone, and Will felt Horus the hawk hit the winged helmet he was holding like a sledgehammer. The force of the impact knocked him forward off the bench, and if he had not had the chinstrap twined round his hand he would have dropped it.

But the straps held, and the force of the hawk's attack and the strength of its talons as it tried to wrench

88

the hat away were so strong that as the hawk flapped upwards again, Will found he was being lifted into the air by the helmet.

He didn't have time to shout or fight back, he just dangled under the hawk and flailed about like the world's least coordinated hang-glider. The hawk lifted him higher, each mighty wing-flap lifting him towards the roof above and making the drop below increasingly deadly.

He got a nasty bang on the side as the hawk flew him into a girder, either by mistake or in an effort to knock him off the helmet. It didn't matter which, really, because it hurt either way, and the impact winded him too much to let him shout for help.

Help, however, was on the way.

Jo had sprung off the bench after him. Betch tried to hold her back, crying, 'Careful, my dear!'

But she shrugged out of his grip and took to the air, the little wings on her sandals whirring as she spiralled upwards, trying to catch up with the hawk.

Will caught a glimpse of her flying, and saw with horror that she had reversed her walking cane so that she was now holding it like a hockey stick, cocked and ready to strike.

He tried to shout 'no' but he was still gasping for

air, and his hands were too busy holding on to the helmet and stopping him falling down to the ground that was now so suddenly and fatally far below him that he couldn't spare one to try and wave her off.

Jo had been good at hockey before she'd hurt her knee. She'd spent hours with him and their dad whacking balls round the field behind the house. If she connected with the hawk there was every chance she'd knock it out, and then it and Will would both plummet to a painful end.

He saw her swipe at the hawk, and luckily the hawk saw it too, as it dropped and avoided the blow.

'Put him down!' she shouted.

Will lurched through the air, spinning now as the helmet straps twisted from the sudden evasive action the hawk was taking.

Will got his breath back.

'Jo!' he shouted. 'No, don't—'

She skated through the air, hot on the hawk's tail, and whacked at it again.

Once more the hawk swooped and avoided the blow, but this time the force of her attack and the follow-through on her swing sent her banging into her brother, sending him off like a spinning pendulum beneath the hawk.

He saw the station whizzing past him in a kind of sick-making blur, and in the blur he caught fragments of things.

He saw Betch waving his hat far below, trying to swat at the hawk as if he was trying to swat a wasp away from a picnic.

He saw Tragedy and Wolfie waving and shouting at something.

He saw a very hard-looking girder brush past his nose, fast and brutal.

Then he saw the giant kissing couple unlock from each other and the big man's hand reach for them like the boom of a crane, missing but coming so close he felt the wind off it as it passed.

'Don't hit it!' Will shouted. 'I'll fall . . .'

And even as the words came out of his mouth he saw a huge rectangle of bronze the size of a church door come flying at them, and in the moment before he was swatted like a fly he realised the big girl was trying to handbag the hawk and he knew he needed to fly left, fast, to avoid it . . .

. . . and he did. His mind, shocked by the hawk's attack, reconnected with the helmet somehow, and he remembered he was able to fly under his own steam. The wings on the helmet thrummed into overdrive.

The handbag sailed past, missing him by millimetres as he flew himself and the still-attached Horus out of the way of its lethal arc.

It was Horus's turn to squawk as it found itself being tugged sideways by the helmet, and then it shrieked as Will's need to get lower and safer took over and the pair of them swooped downwards in a steep parabola, glancing off the brickwork on the side of the station with another painful thump.

The impact knocked Will's fingers loose from the straps and he tumbled to the shiny floor of the concourse, landing with all the airborne elegance of a bag of spanners. His momentum sent him careening towards the end wall of the station as he scrabbled desperately to slow himself.

He conspired to get his feet facing forward, so was able to take some of the impact by bending his knees, but he still managed to bite his tongue painfully as the jarring shock went through his whole frame.

'Will!' shouted Jo, flying in from above him.

'Gurg!' he said, gasping for breath. 'Gnah . . . Stay back!'

Horus landed on the ground in front of him in a clash of stone and bronze, the helmet held in its nastily hooked little beak. It blinked at him and then jerked its head sideways, letting go of the helmet so that it frisbeed off into the crowd of frozen travellers, where it hit a suitcase and spun to the floor with a clatter.

The hawk blinked again, the blue disc around its eye focused on him. It stepped slowly forward, its obsidian talons scraping on the stone.

Will was groggily trying to get to his feet and then he froze, trying to work out which way to jump.

And then, just as the hawk lunged for him and he scuttled backwards . . .

. . . Betch leapt forward and stamped his foot down on the hawk's tail, pinning it in place.

The hawk had time to squawk in outrage at this assault on his dignity and try to get airborne, but not quite enough time to avoid Betch's hat, which the resourceful poet slapped down over its head with both hands.

'Groark!' said Horus.

And then it went as limp as a ragdoll.

'Wow!' said Will.

'Hood a hawk and it goes as calm as a baby,' grinned Betch, his smile making him look much younger. 'Though I never found babies *especially* good at being calm. Perhaps I jiggled them too much . . .'

WHO ARE YOU?

Bast's voice boomed around the station, strangely muffled yet loud enough to stop everyone in their tracks.

Jo landed next to Will and reached out a hand.

'I'm fine,' he said.

WHO ARE YOU?

The cat's voice was more insistent.

'That's the cat,' said Jo. 'That's Bast.'

Everyone looked around, tensed and ready to fight or flee, depending on where the cat was and who she was with. But there was no sign of her.

'Where?' said Tragedy, his voice quavering a little.

Betch coughed.

The Clocker pointed at Betch's pork-pie hat, which the middle-aged poet was still holding down over the hawk with both hands.

'Cat in the hat,' he said.

# 8

## The Cat in the Hat

The cat was not in the hat. Obviously.

The hat was full of a very angry stone hawk's head. A hawk under the distinct impression that it was at least the Eye of the god Horus, if not an actual manifestation of said god himself. There was no room for a cat as well.

The truth was stranger than that.

It took them a few moments to arrange things so that they could make everything secure enough to see exactly how much stranger, but it was time well spent. Angry stone hawks with sharp eyes and even sharper beaks and talons are not to be taken lightly; the Clocker's ingenuity and cache of surprisingly useful tools and supplies helped make things safe enough to risk unhooding the hawk.

He worked fast and efficiently, his fingers nimbly twisting waxed twine around the hawk's legs, hobbling it. Then he did the same with its wings using some jeweller's wire, lashing them to the body with a criss-cross binding that parcelled it up so that it could not possibly fly away. Only then did he allow Betch to gingerly lift the hat and reveal the head: the eyes were shut, and the hawk looked as if it was sleeping, but as soon as it was fully unhooded, the eyes opened and blinked angrily, a bright-blue rim of blue light blazing round them in a perfect pair of circles.

The hawk struggled against its bindings, but it only managed to hop a little and fall on its side.

Jo couldn't help but feel bad for it. What had once been terrifying death-from-the-air was now an undignified and rather helpless-looking bundle.

Betch must have felt the same, because he leaned over, gingerly picked the bird up and put it back on its talon-feet, moving his hands away just in time to avoid a sharp and – in the circumstances – ungrateful peck.

Then, after a certain amount of visible struggling against its bonds, the hawk settled down and looked at them. The blue-ringed eye moved from one to the other in an unsettlingly precise way as if – Jo thought – it was taking a mental picture of each of its enemies and filing it away for later action.

Will was getting exactly the same impression, but

made worse by the fact that the Eye of Horus finished its precise cataloguing by staring at him for an uncomfortably longer time than any of the others.

Maybe it was being singled out like this, or perhaps it was because no one had taken the time to ask how badly bruised and banged up he was after his recent ordeal, but he began to feel that old familiar anger building up inside him. It was the feeling of things being not being fair in a way he couldn't quite put his finger on that led to this frustration. Oddly, it was all the worse because he knew it was an irrational thing, because Jo had been through as much if not more than he had. But the old sense of angry resentment was definitely spiking, and though part of him could rationally push it away, another part of him somehow held on to it.

Perhaps it was because he had been scared and running for so long. Fighting the sapping effect of prolonged fear will make you cling to anything that gives you the least bit of energy, even if it's just raw and unjustified anger. And Will knew that without the anger to fuel him, he was pretty much running on empty.

He glared at Horus as all these thoughts swirled through his head.

The eye, the pitiless hunter's eye, did not blink. But the beak opened.

WHAT ARE YOU, BOY, AND WHY DO YOU MOVE?

Bast's voice came booming out of the hawk.

Will gulped, steeling himself, and stared back into the hawk's eye.

His first instinct was to wonder why it couldn't have picked on Jo, but then with a shudder he realised he could see the cat peering out at him from the ring of blue light, as if the eyeball was a kind of screen showing the interior of the museum.

Extraordinary though it was, he was less interested that he could see the cat than he was chilled by the fact that Bast could not only control the stone hawk, but see him, Will, too.

WHAT ARE YOU?

'What are *you*?' said Will. 'And where is our mum?'

WHAT IS A MUM?

'Our mother,' said Jo, coming to peer at the cat over Will's shoulder.

And now, because he was definitely in the grip of a kind of cross-grained mulishness, Will resented her for sticking her nose into his conversation, where a moment ago he had been wishing the cat had chosen to speak to her in the first place.

He tried to ride the irrational anger and keep calm. Perhaps he'd taken a bigger bang to the head than he'd thought.

YOUR MOTHER? said Bast innocently.

'Yes,' said Will. 'She's . . .'

And then he stopped talking and the only sound seemed to be his heart whacking against the inside of his ribcage and Jo gasping in shock as Bast stepped back, and they saw their mother, frozen and slack-faced behind the cat, held in place by two of the cat-women warrior-statues.

OH. THIS IS HER?

Will's mouth was suddenly too dry and gummy to speak. His sister leaned over his shoulder.

'Don't hurt her. Don't you dare hurt her . . .'

Her voice was raw and ragged.

OR WHAT?

'Or I'll hurt *you*.'

YOU WOULD FIGHT ME?

'To save our mum?' said Will. 'I'd fight anyone.'

The cat licked her paws, as if thinking about what he'd just said.

IS THAT A CHALLENGE?

'It's a promise,' said Jo. 'If it's a fair fight . . .'

'Even if it's unfair,' she muttered under her breath.

'And no magic,' said Will.

THEN I ACCEPT.

Will and Jo stared at each other.

'Hang on . . .' said Jo.

'What?' said Will.

I ACCEPT THE CHALLENGE.

IF YOU CAN DEFEAT ME OR MY CHAMPION THEN I WILL EXCHANGE YOUR MOTHER FOR MY HAWK. BUT IF YOU LOSE, THEN YOU GIVE ME THE SECRET OF YOUR MAGIC TALISMAN. YOU GIVE ME THE TALISMAN ITSELF.

'Wait,' said Betch. 'Its champion?'

'What champion?' said Will. Things were moving faster than he was anywhere near comfortable with.

I CANNOT FIGHT, said Bast, making her voice sound uncharacteristically soothing. I AM JUST A SMALL CAT.

'Thought you were the Mighty Bast,' said Jo, leaning in past Will again.

The cat blinked slowly back at her.

YOU ASKED FOR A FAIR FIGHT AND NO MAGIC, purred Bast. I GAVE YOU THAT. YOU SHOULD GIVE ME THIS. IT IS ONLY FAIR.

'When an obvious cheat and sneak like that blasted cat starts talking about being fair, it's usually a good time to watch your back,' said Betch.

'You might choose something massive though,' said Will. 'You've got a lot of choice in there.'

He was thinking of all the giant statues he remembered inside the museum, things that could crush a man-sized statue without trying.

FINE. YOU MAY CHOOSE A STATUE AS YOUR CHAMPION TOO, said Bast. There was a smirk in the cat's voice. IF YOU CAN FIND ONE TO FIGHT FOR YOU. THERE ARE EVEN MORE STATUES OUT THERE, AFTER ALL. THE HAWK HAS SHOWN ME THAT.

Will put his hand over the hawk's eye and winked at Jo. She looked back, not getting it.

He took his hand off the eye and looked into Bast's waiting face.

'Is that your best offer?' he said.

IT IS FAIR, said Bast. BUT I DO NOT HAVE TIME TO WASTE. THE OFFER ENDS AT SUNDOWN.

'Er,' coughed the Clocker, leaning in and putting his own hand over the hawk's eye. 'Just to say. Betch right. Cat sharp type. Sharp types never make deal unless in their own favour. Word to wise, d'you see?'

He smiled nervously at them both, bobbed his head and unblinkered the eye of Horus.

Jo whispered to Will, 'If we win and we get Mum, London's still going to be frozen, no?'

He looked at her. She dug him in the ribs.

'That's still bad. Make it part of the deal now, before we agree.'

Will swallowed and looked back at the cat. It really was like watching a little round TV screen, except somehow what you saw was a lot bigger than the circumference of the eye. What was even more disconcerting was the fact that Bast was clearly leaning closer on the other side of the connection, trying to hear what they were saying. The cat was so close she was really all eye. She hissed and leaned back, becoming smaller in the lens again.

WHAT ARE YOU CHILDREN WHISPERING ABOUT?

'Nothing for you to know,' said Will, 'or we wouldn't have been whispering, would we?'

I DON'T LIKE CHILDREN, said Bast.

'Well,' said Will. 'The feeling's mutual. I never liked cats. They're like dogs without personalities.'

'Will!' Jo whispered urgently. 'Not the time! Play it cool.'

He shrugged off her hand in irritation, and fake-smiled into the lens as he cleared his throat again.

'To be clear about the deal: if we win, we get our mum, right?' he said, 'and when . . . if that happens, everything goes back to normal, right?'

Bast cocked her head as if thinking.

VERY WELL. WHY NOT? OF COURSE.

'I don't trust it,' said Jo. 'It looks really shifty.'

'I know,' whispered Will. 'But I've got a plan.'

'Yeah but slow down,' Jo said. 'I mean, we need to think this through, like how's this going to affect Mum. She'll probably go mad when she sees all this with no warning,' she added. 'I would. You would. She'll think she's hallucinating. She might have a heart attack with the shock. She might have a stroke. She might have a whatever it's called and be catatonic anyway! Shock can do terrible things, shock can! We need to think about this.'

'Jo, we'll be there to help her when it comes to that,' said Will.

Then he looked at Bast and nodded.

'Deal.'

Jo stared at him.

'Wait!' she said. 'What did you just do?'

'You were losing it,' he said.

'You just made the deal?' she said, looking like he'd slapped her.

HE DID, purred the cat.

'I had to,' said Will.

'Without checking with me?' said Jo in disbelief. 'We agreed—'

'You were losing it,' he repeated. 'You were starting to babble. It was the right thing to do.'

She stared at him. He wondered if she was going to shout. Or slap. Or walk off. Instead she just looked blank. And now, just when he could have done with that anger as a bit of a shield against feeling and about how lost she suddenly appeared to be, it deserted him.

'I'm sorry,' he said. 'But you were babbling. I had to make the call.'

Her eyes gave him nothing. She looked lost. He was used to a lot of expressions flying across her normally animated face, but this was not one he was used to.

A DEAL IS A DEAL, said the cat. AND I CHOOSE AS MY CHAMPION MIGHTY SEKHMET, SCOURGE OF THE DESERT, THE WARRIOR WHO NO SINGLE MAN HAS EVER – CAN EVER – BEAT!

The satisfaction in the cat's voice rubbed salt in the wound, rekindling a little of that anger.

'See?' said Jo. 'It was cheating . . .'

She felt too battered by despair and frustration to carry on.

A DEAL IS A DEAL, repeated Bast.

'It is,' spat Will. 'So you'd better get ready to get your nasty cat-self thoroughly beaten. Now, go away.'

He pulled the hat back over the hawk's head and it went limp as abruptly as if he'd thrown a switch.

'Well,' said Betch, looking at the Clocker. 'There's a thing.'

'Thing indeed,' agreed the Clocker. 'Though whether good thing or bad thing, time will tell.'

'Then I'm sure you'll be the first to know,' said Betch, tightly buttoning his flapping raincoat in a businesslike fashion. 'Let's try not to be late for the Bridge Moot. We have lots to tell them.'

Will looked at Jo.

'We said we'd stay together,' she said, so tired she couldn't even put much energy into her anger.

'We are together,' he smiled. 'Come on, have a little faith!'

'We said we'd make all decisions together too,' she said. 'I mean—'

'Give me some credit,' he said, reaching into his pocket.

'Why?' she said. 'What have you done other than make things worse?'

'I fooled it,' said Will. 'Or her, whatever that cat thing is. He, she or it thinks it's got us beat because it can choose any statue it likes to fight our champion, right?'

'How does that help us?' said Jo.

'But we can use a statue as OUR champion too,' he said.

'Which would be great if the cat hadn't cursed all the soldier-statues. You know, the ones that are actually good at fighting, the ones who know how to use weapons and other useful things like that. It'd be great if it hadn't frozen them, but you know what, genius brother?' she said. 'The cat *did* do that. So who exactly do you suggest we choose for our mighty champion to fight whatever dragon or god-knows-what she has up her sleeve? Politicians? Angels? Wolfie? Tragedy? Artists? Poets?'

Betch coughed.

'Sorry,' said Jo. 'But I don't think you're probably much good at fighting, are you?'

'Not the punching or stabbing kind of fighting, no,'

said Betch. 'But I'm quite good at thinking, and half a fight takes place in the mind, is what they say.'

'Maybe,' she said. 'But it's not the half that wins one, is it? It's the stabby, punchy part that decides in the end. We need a soldier . . . but we can't use one.'

'Yes we can,' said Will, pulling the thing he'd been fishing for out of his pocket.

It was the scarab bracelet.

'This breaks the curse, remember?'

He grinned.

'That's my plan. That's how we fooled the cat. How *I* fooled the cat. We go and put it on the Fusilier. He fought about six dragons and was winning until he sacrificed himself to save me. I reckon he can beat one measly champion—'

'What are you doing?' said a girl's voice.

They looked up and saw Ariel had flown in and was hovering above them. Betch smiled and waved.

'Hello, my lovely, where have you popped in from?'

'Parts north,' she said. 'And why aren't you going to the Bridge Moot? You're going to be late. You too, Clocker.'

Betch beamed at her and then leaned down and spoke to Will and Jo.

'Isn't she a corker? Always lifts my old heart to

see her, it does. I've always had a weakness for Golden Girls.'

'Golden Girls?' said Jo. She wasn't a Golden Girl, she knew that. She was a tired, aching and – after her passage through the underground tunnels and rooftops of London – definitely grubby girl.

'Furnished and burnished by the sun,' said Betch, grinning at Ariel, who was enjoying the attention but pretending not to in a rather unconvincing way.

'Now, hurry up. If you two can take the Clocker, I'll carry Betch,' she said. 'The Moot's about to begin. Tower Bridge, right?'

'Right,' said Will, strapping on the winged helmet. He was sure that between Jo and himself they could manage to carry the thin man.

'We're just going to make one short stop on the way. I'm going to free the Fusilier, and then that cat's going to get a sharp surprise, right where it hurts.'

# 9

## *Spilt Milk*

The damaged Sphinx had left the museum and walked carefully through the herd of animal statues that now seemed to mill endlessly and aimlessly around it. Or, in fact, not entirely aimlessly, it noted: as they grudgingly made room for it, there was a sullen air of something close to threat.

It wasn't aimed at it. It was a Sphinx, after all, and above such things. It was more the general rumble of a mob. A mob is a different thing to a crowd. A crowd is just a large number of people or, in this case, animals. It has no real intent. Mobs, on the other hand, are crowds with attitude. A mob is subject to hidden tides of emotion and intent that seem to ebb and flow at will. The dangerous thing about a crowd with attitude is that no one is necessarily in charge of it. It just seems to build, like static electricity, as if it's caused by the friction of so many beings crowded into one space. Threat, that was the attitude the Sphinx felt as it passed; silent currents of menace, not aimed at it specifically, but just there beneath the surface waiting to lash out if the right provocation occurred.

A crowd is just a crowd, but a mob is trouble waiting to happen.

As if to prove this, a large bronze kudu failed to join the other statues moving to clear a path for the Sphinx. The antelope was nearly as tall as the Sphinx, being an oversized statue, and its sharp horns lowered a fraction as it got closer.

The Sphinx didn't slow or waver. It just walked regally forward, calm as ever, and at the last moment the kudu snorted, pawed the ground . . . and stepped away.

'Good decision,' murmured the Sphinx as it passed. 'Very good decision.'

It walked onwards towards the river, a stately feline colossus moving through the frozen pedestrians, who were all now rimed with blue hoarfrost. It looked at them as it passed, and at one point actually stopped and reached out one of its giant paws to touch a woman who was caught in the act of stepping off a bus.

The great paw gently rested against the static figure, and then the Sphinx shivered a little at the cold coming off the small human figure. The Sphinx dropped its head and looked closely into the unmoving face in front of it.

Then it stepped back and moved on, and the only sign that it might have been affected by what it had seen and felt was that its tail now swished slowly from side to side, as if dissipating some irritation.

It reached the jutting column of Cleopatra's Needle, and walked past its twin, who was lying on its usual plinth, seemingly oblivious as it watched the afternoon sunlight on the Thames beyond the embankment wall.

However, as it paused and looked at its own plinth, but did not climb back on it, the other Sphinx spoke softly.

'And what has upset you, sister?'

'Nothing,' it replied.

'What kind of nothing?' said the other.

There was no reply, and since neither moved and the city was frozen, the silence that followed was profound and unbroken.

In fact, the only things that moved were the shadows that the weak sun threw across the face of the buildings and the pavement beside them. When those shadows had lengthened, the damaged Sphinx stepped away from its plinth and looked directly over the parapet and down into the river.

'I might have done a bad thing,' it said. 'Seeing someone from the past come back unexpectedly . . . thinking about the consequences . . . I don't know. Made me think I did a bad thing. Yes.'

The other Sphinx said nothing. But the silence itself was a question.

'I don't know how to balance it,' said the one looking into the Thames as if it held solutions just below the surface of the water. 'And . . .'

It shook herself and stopped talking. And then after a while it turned from the river that was giving it no answers and walked away.

'And?' said her sister, watching it go. 'And?'

'This is a riddle that I cannot untangle, this business between humans and statues and this new old thing Bast. But there is one statue that has always been good at understanding the few humans who've ever seen us as we are. He might be able to help.'

'The Gunner?' said the watching Sphinx

'The Gunner,' sighed the walking one over its shoulder. 'But he's a soldier, of course, so the one person who might be able to help me unriddle this is frozen. Still, I think I'll go and get him anyway. Everything can change. No harm in being prepared.'

# 10

## Best-laid Plans

It turned out that the Clocker was every bit as light as Will had thought. He and Jo each took a hand, and after an ungainly lift-off found that they could easily fly and carry him with them, especially once they'd got the hang of matching speeds with each other.

The Clocker's dangling tools jingled as they flew out of the end of the train-shed and turned south, towards Holborn. And although they followed Ariel's advice, which was to stay low and fly along the streets where possible so as not to attract more attention, Will felt his heart soaring as they headed towards the Fusilier, which was the stop he had insisted on making before they joined the others at the Bridge Moot. He had never seen anyone fight as well or as doggedly as the Fusilier, and if the means of freeing their mother was to be a fight between champions, he really couldn't imagine a better one than the tough and wiry World War One veteran. He knew the elation buoying him up was a reaction to the anger and frustration he'd been swamped by earlier, before he'd realised how to beat the cat, and he felt good about it. After all, it was about time things started to take a turn for the better.

'What?' said Jo, craning to look at him as they sped through the air over the frozen rooftops of the cars and buses below. 'What turn?' she said. 'I thought we were heading south?'

He realised he'd been talking out loud to himself.

'Was just saying things were taking a turn for the better,' he said.

'Hope you're right,' she said.

'I am,' he said, grinning and pointing at the approaching intersection ahead of them. 'But we go left here.'

The Clocker kept silent, his face locked in a kind of perma-grin as the air flew past him. Jo had the sense that he didn't much like this flying sensation but was too kind or polite to mention it.

'You OK?' she said, squeezing his hand. Her mother always told them that the way to stop feeling bad about something was to check on those around them and try to think how they felt instead. He turned to look at her as they angled left and carried on flying.

'Tip-top,' he said, jerking his head in a nod. Then he pointed with his chin at the unmoving people below. 'Those poor people? Not. See blue glow? Bad thing. Getting worse.'

Will and Jo looked at the blueness that covered the unmoving crowds below like a sinister hoarfrost. It was certainly deeper and thicker than it had been.

If they had been looking up instead of down, they would have noticed that despite the fact they'd been following Ariel's advice, they had been noticed by something that was also in the sly.

Only this time they would have seen not a hawk or a winged dragon, but something shinier, smaller and much more sinister.

One of the gilded soup-plate-sized mosquitoes that had peeled off the side of the School of Hygiene and Tropical Medicine and attacked them earlier was still looking for them. And it was not flying alone. It was carrying one of the matching gilded bedbugs underneath it, like a bomb. And both the bug and the mosquito saw the strange trio flying below them, and very quietly adjusted the angle of their flight to shadow them, drifting into place, quite low, and just behind them. In their blind spot.

Will and Jo were too focused on the blue-rimmed

pedestrians below them to notice they were, once again, hunter's prey.

'That's bad magic, isn't it?' said Jo.

To her surprise the Clocker snorted.

'Magic. No such thing. Magic smoke and mirrors. Abracadabra. Hocus-pocus. Flimflam for fools.'

Will and Jo exchanged a look.

'Er. What is it then, if it's not magic?' said Will.

It certainly looked like magic as far as he was concerned.

'Curse,' said the Clocker. 'Magic mumbo jumbo. Curses real.'

'But Tragedy said the Bridge Moot was being held on the river because bad magic couldn't work over flowing water,' said Jo. 'He did say that, right, Will?'

Will nodded.

'Tragedy a child,' said the Clocker. 'Believe fairy tales. Though true that new curse can't take over water. Magic just his way of understanding. Old wives' tales.'

Jo thought the difference between a curse and magic was, in the circumstances, so little that it wasn't worth talking about, but before she could find a way to say it that wasn't somehow too rude, Will had pointed and begin to slow and drop lower. She lost her train of thought as they concentrated on coming in to land without crashing into the tall stone plinth in the middle of the street on which stood the familiar and – she had to admit – reassuring silhouette of the Fusilier with rifle and long bayonet at the ready.

They came to an ungainly halt on the road, and let go of the Clocker's hands at more or less the same time. He stumbled onwards, windmilling his arms to get his balance, and then tripped slightly on the raised kerb before stopping himself with his palms against the plinth.

'Well,' he said, turning and dusting himself off. 'Flying an adventure. But firm ground more reliable.'

He looked at Will and then up at the frozen statue above them.

'You too short.'

He turned his back to the stone, leaned against it and then interlaced his fingers, joining his two hands to make a stirrup. He smiled encouragingly at Will.

'Give you a boost.'

'No need,' said Will. 'I can fly!'

'Of course,' said the Clocker. 'Stupid me. Was f—'

The golden mosquito chose that moment to attack, buzzing in and dropping the bed bug like a bomb.

Or rather, like something worse than an actual bomb that explodes, because although bombs have

118

been invented that go bang with unimaginable destructive power, no one has invented a bomb that has too many flailing grippy little legs that smack into people's faces and then hold tightly on, smothering them and stopping them breathe – which is just what the giant bed bug did to the Clocker.

The Clocker had no time to say anything more than:

'Gnarfff!'

And then he was struggling frantically to get the gilded gag off his face so that he could gasp a new breath before passing out. His head jerked wildly from side to side as he tugged this way and that, but he was unable to rip his mouth and nose free from the tenacious insect.

Without thinking, Jo leapt to his aid, swooping in and grabbing the bug. It pulsed horribly under her fingers, but even though she got her knees in between herself and the Clocker and used all of her body strength to help him try to wrench it clear, it just dug in with its nasty little legs and held on like a limpet.

Will flew straight up to the Fusilier and tried to fix his mother's scarab bracelet around the statue's unmoving wrists, but he was trying too hard and kept fumbling.

He could hear the grunts and struggles of the fight below him, and then there was a yelp and he looked down quickly, horrified to see that the Clocker had fallen back into the road and landed on Jo. As she rolled him over he saw that the bug was still in place.

'Will!' shouted Jo, without looking round. 'Need some help here!'

'I'm trying!' he yelled, hearing the panic rip through his normal voice, making it shriller than it normally was.

'Try harder!' she shouted. He saw the muscles in her back bunch as she refused to stop pulling at the bug. The Clocker's hands were no longer helping her, but slapping feebly at the insect as his strength and consciousness began to drain from him.

Will took a fast breath, tried to clear his mind and then calmly snapped the scarab bracelet in place. This time he didn't fumble it.

The Fusilier immediately changed, the cold bronze becoming no less hard but somehow soft at the same time, in the way Will had noted before.

'Oi! Shift out the way,' came a familiar gritty voice.

The Fusilier pushed Will aside and shouldered his rifle in one fast movement.

In Will's mind, at least later when he tried to

remember exactly what had happened next, everything went slow, yet simultaneously seemed to happen very fast.

Jo roared.

There was no other word for it.

She roared like a weightlifter, her voice ragged and unnaturally low, as if using every last bit of her strength was tearing some last bit of animal power from her small body.

And it worked.

There was a kid of 'pop', and the bug was suddenly free as she tore it loose.

She let go, tossing it spinning over her shoulder.

Straight towards Will and the Fusilier.

Will saw its little legs thrashing angrily as it spun towards him.

He heard it chittering in frustration.

And then he saw the Fusilier lunge forward and spear it with the long sword-bayonet attached to his rifle.

'Gotcher, nasty little blighter,' he grunted.

Will took a breath and looked down to see the Clocker spluttering and taking one of his own. Will was about to smile when he saw the look of panic on Jo's face.

He followed her eyeline and saw what she was seeing.

The gilded mosquito came howling angrily towards her, all of its six spindly legs looking as sharp as stilettos, its blood-sucking nose aimed at her face like a lance.

And her foot was stuck under the Clocker.

She couldn't get out of the way in time.

And Will couldn't get to her fast enough to help.

At the same moment this horrible realisation hit him, half a second before the mosquito hit her, the Fusilier fired his gun.

The shot hit the bug that was inconveniently kebabed on the bayonet clipped beneath the barrel and took it with it, the force of the projectile blowing the bug and the bullet into the mosquito, and shattering both of them into gilded splinters before any harm came to Jo.

'Wow,' said Will, his ears ringing from the detonation. 'Nice shot!'

Jo turned her head and looked at them. Her eyes were wide with shock. It was too soon for relief to flow into them in its place, but then she grinned.

'Thanks,' she said. 'You saved me.'

'Was your brother this time, I reckon,' said the Fusilier, looking down at the bracelet round his wrist.

'This little wossname seems to lift the curse, don't it?'

The Clocker allowed Jo to help him to his feet.

'Thank you. All of you. You saved me. Everlastingly indebted.' He coughed and spluttered, then held up a shaking bony finger with one hand while he dived the other into a waistcoat pocket and came out with a surprisingly bright-green and red polka-dot handkerchief and blew his nose. 'Sorry. Vile experience. Foul taste in mouth. Taste of insect.'

He put away the handkerchief and retrieved a small paper bag from another pocket. He popped something into his mouth and offered the bag to the children.

'Humbug?' he said.

'What?' said Will.

'It's a mint,' said the Fusilier.

'Take away the taste,' agreed the Clocker.

They each took a boiled sweet and put it in their mouth. The Fusilier stayed up on his plinth and didn't take one.

'Been in his pocket for couple of hundred years,' he said, sucking in his breath and nodding at Will, who was tasting mint and sugar and something a bit stale all at the same time. 'You're a better man than I am, Gunga Din.'

'I'm not,' said Will. 'That's the point.'

'What's the point?' said the Fusilier.

'The point of why we're here,' said Will, his voice gaining strength now the immediate peril was over. In fact, he felt even better about his plan now he'd seen how calmly and clinically the Fusilier had dealt with the flying insects.

'We need a champion,' said Jo. Will saw she'd quietly removed the humbug and was holding it at her side where the Clocker couldn't see it. She made a 'yuck' face at him. He could taste the humbug in his own mouth. The mint had worn quickly off and the sugar tasted a little rancid. But he saw the Clocker smiling brightly up at him from just behind her, and felt it'd be rude to spit it out quite so obviously.

'A champion?' said the Fusilier. 'What d'you need a champion for?'

Will and Jo took it in turns to tell him about the deal they'd made with Bast, about a trial by combat that would allow them to free their mother if they or their champion won, and about how Will had realised the cat thought they wouldn't be able to use a real soldier because of her curse. And then he pointed at the scarab bracelet around the Fusilier's wrist.

'And see, that's why we came, to free you from the curse, to let you move again and so you could come and fight for us.'

He saw the Fusilier grimace, which stopped him mid-flow. He was hit by a sudden doubt, an awareness of what he was asking the soldier to do, to risk, for them.

Jo caught the look and was obviously thinking the same thing because she said, 'If you'd be willing to fight for us, for our mum. I mean, I know she's not your mum, but we do need a champion of some sort and you've, well, really you've been brilliant so far . . .'

And she dried up too, catching something odd about the Fusilier's body language.

'I mean,' said Will. 'I mean – we mean – that we'd be grateful if you would agree to help us, but we'd think no worse—'

'NOBODY would think any worse of you if you didn't volunteer,' said Jo earnestly. 'We know it's a lot to ask.'

The Fusilier grimaced again and held his hand up to stop them.

'Whoa there,' he said. 'I'd fight for you. Hell, I'd fight for all of us if I could, anywhere and any time you like, if it would stop this unnaturalness what's got the whole city froze up like this. But I can't . . .'

'What?' said Will. He felt like he'd been punched again. 'But—'

'Not a matter of not wanting to,' said the Fusilier. 'I mean, your bracelet – it's strong enough to break the bit of the curse as what's frozen me, but it's not strong enough to get me free of my plinth. Look . . .'

He made that grimace again and Will realised that he had been trying to move his feet.

'Can't budge off this perishing perch I'm on,' said the Fusilier. 'Like my boots is stuck in concrete. Sorry, but that's the truth of it.'

Will stared at him.

'Maybe if I put the bracelet round your ankle?' he said.

'Well, I dunno. Go on, try it,' said the Fusilier. 'Can't do any harm.'

Will did try it, and managed to do so without fumbling at all this time. The Fusilier strained and yanked at his feet but all that did was confirm that he'd told the truth about them being stuck fast. He hadn't been right about 'trying not doing any harm' though, because Will felt the bottom falling out of his world with every futile tug: he'd not only overestimated his own cleverness, he'd betrayed their mother again.

126

'Sorry, chum,' said the Fusilier. 'Ain't going to work. I'm planted good an' proper.'

'What do we do now?' said Will.

'Go to the Bridge Moot,' said the Clocker, shifting his weight uncomfortably from foot to foot. 'We're late as it is. First time for me. Being late.'

'Bridge Moot?' said the Fusilier. 'Good idea. Lot of handy statues there, even if they ain't in uniform. Someone will have a plan, sure as guns.'

He smiled just a little too brightly, thought Will, like he was trying to make the best of a bad job.

Will looked down at Jo.

'I'm sorry,' he said. 'I'm really sorry.'

'Is that going to save Mum?' she said, face tight as a drum.

'No,' he said.

'Then be sorry later,' she said. 'After we've rescued her. For now, save your energy and keep thinking how we're going to make that happen.'

She shifted her gaze to the Fusilier.

'Thank you for trying,' she said. 'And thank you for saving me.'

The Fusilier raised his hand to the brim of his tin hat, half a wave, half a salute.

'No trouble, miss. Now, you get on out of here.

Going to make Old Clock there lose his name if you're really late, ain'tcha?'

He slapped Will on the back. And then leaned in and spoke quietly, just to him.

'Chin up, mate. Don't let that b****** cat grind you down. Tough little pair you are, you and your sister. You ain't beat yet, not by a long chalk.'

Will nodded and found he couldn't speak round the lump in his throat. He flew down and took the Clocker's hand, and then he and Jo flew towards the river.

'Chins up, the lot of you!' shouted the Fusilier, dwindling into miniature in the streetscape they were leaving behind them. 'And never, ever say die!'

Will kept his mouth shut as they flew on. But the thought of what would happen if they didn't come up with a new plan now seemed to tug at him like lead boots, trying to pull him back down to earth.

# 11

## Bridge Moot

As they flew along the Thames, the familiar silhouette of Tower Bridge grew in front of them, blocking their way, like a gateway to the world beyond London, a world that might be normal, a world that might not be frozen.

They were both beginning to feel less and less connected to the memory of such a world. Even the extraordinary can begin to seem humdrum if you're trapped in it for long enough, thought Jo. Her bad leg was twinging badly: she'd managed to twist it while trying to tug herself free of the Clocker when he fell on her. If they'd had time she would have tried to find some painkillers from a supermarket or a chemist's, but things were happening too fast. And on top of that she was feeling angry with Will for making the deal with the cat before he'd found out that his plan for freeing the Fusilier from the curse was going to be only partially successful.

And of course in this case 'partially' meant 'not at all'. But she knew that while going on at him about it might help her vent her frustration, it wouldn't help them solve their problem. So, clenching her teeth against the ache in her bad knee also kept words inside her that were best not let out at all.

As they got closer, Will realised the bridge itself didn't appear at all normal: it was crowded with what looked like every non-military and non-animal statue in London. He hadn't realised exactly how many of those there were, but the entire length and breadth of the roadway was crammed with a heaving mass of kings and queens and poets and explorers and sailors and nymphs, and all manner of others in every costume you could imagine – including no costume at all for the underdressed classical and allegorical statues mixing unconcernedly with the others.

The top span of the bridge was festooned with so many angels and Victories and other flying statues circling and hovering around it that it looked like a cross between a giant Christmas garland and a bat colony.

A shout went up from the roadway where the statue of a sea captain had spotted them through his telescope. All the statues were in such a disorganised mess that

very few of them could actually see at what, or even where, he was looking, but a thunderous stone Neptune towered over them and pointed his trident.

'There!' he said. 'Look to the west; here come the saviours!'

The whole mass of statues, land-bound and airborne, erupted into a raucous cacophony of hurrahs and whooping and whistling, which only made things worse from Will's point of view because it suggested Betch and Ariel, or Tragedy and Wolfie, had already spilled the beans about his now abortive plans.

As they dropped down onto a space hurriedly cleared for them on one of the bridge islands, all his worst fears were realised as Tragedy tumbled out of the crowd with a big grin on his face, followed by Ariel, whose hopeful smile was, if possible, making her shine even more brightly than normal.

'Where's the Fusilier?' she said. 'Shall I go and whisk him here?'

Will cleared his throat. He seemed to be surrounded by hopeful smiles. He'd never seen anything so dispiriting. And he didn't know how to break it to them. He cleared his throat, wishing that clearing his head was as easy.

'Er . . .' he said.

'It won't work,' said Jo. 'Sorry, but the scarab bracelet made the Fusilier able to move again, but it wasn't powerful enough to counter the bit of the curse that keeps him stuck on his plinth.'

'Huh,' said Tragedy, deflating like a punctured balloon. He plonked down into a sitting position on the pavement. 'So much for that then.'

The statues started mumbling and talking to each other. All the hopeful eyes now turned away, and only looked at the two children in short, snatched glances when they thought they weren't being observed.

'Hero to zero in nothing flat,' said Will.

'Stop feeling sorry for yourself,' said Jo.

'I'm not,' he said. 'I feel sorry for having got their hopes up. I feel sorry for not letting you help make the decision about the deal. And most of all I feel sorry for Mum and all the people stuck by the cat's spell.'

He swept his hand around the view, which was, from this vantage point, a tremendous vista of the city. 'I feel sorry for all this. I don't have enough room to feel sorry for myself. Like you said, maybe that comes later.'

Something pawed at his leg. He looked down.

It was Filax, and his tail was thumping. He held Wolfie's bow in his mouth.

'Vunderful dog!' cried the small *wunderkind* as he burst through the crowd and took it from him. 'If I had a thousand bones I vould shower you viz zem!'

Will scratched Filax's head and the tail thumped even faster. Then the dog began to bark urgently.

Happy came through the crowd, her way made easy by Guy the Gorilla walking ahead of her like a steamroller. She knelt by Filax's side and listened. The dog finished barking, licked her face and looked up at Will and Jo eagerly.

'Your mother is in the museum. In the Egyptian Gallery. But it's all guarded by – well, he said dragons and lions and, er, warriors with lions' heads. But he can sneak you in the back way if you like.'

Filax woofed again.

'He says your mother is fine. But Bast has her watched all the time.'

Will and Jo exchanged a look.

'Should we try and sneak in?' said Will. 'Yeah, maybe we should . . .'

'How would that work once we were in there?' said Jo. 'We don't know what's inside. How can we plan how to deal with it if we don't know even that?'

'I could sneak in with Filax and scout it out,' he said. 'Maybe . . .'

'Before sunset?' she said. 'Because that's the deadline, isn't it?'

Betch stepped out of the crowd and whispered something to the Clocker. The Clocker nodded.

'Could be,' he said. 'Curses come crooked like that.'

'Like what?' said Will.

Betch came over and looked down at him with a smile that was both kind and, in the circumstances, more than welcome.

'Would it help you to feel better if I told you that your plan might well not have worked anyway, even if the bracelet had allowed the poor old Fusilier to step off his plinth?'

'I don't think so,' said Will.

'Go on,' said Jo, stepping closer.

'Well,' said Betch. 'Maybe I read too much into things. In fact, maybe I just read too much, full stop. But one of the stories I remember reading had this old prophecy in it and it led to a sort of surprise, and it reminded me – the cat did – of that book when it started boasting.'

'When it boasted?' said Will. 'What bit? It boasts about everything. It's all boast, far as I can see.'

'Yeah,' said Jo. 'Cat should be called Boast, not Bast.'

'The bit I mean is when it boasted that its champion couldn't be beaten by a single man.'

'Which is why I chose a bronze statue – not just a man – and a soldier too, which the cat didn't know I was going to be able to free,' said Will. 'I mean, until I found out I couldn't.'

'I think it's more than that, and I've been chatting to some of the more mythologically minded statues here, telling them that the cat couldn't help taunting you,' said Betch. 'Cats are cruel, you see. The cat was hiding a barb for the future in its boast.'

'Explain,' said Jo.

'I think it said that because the champion it chooses is one that cannot be beaten by a man, I think it can only be beaten by a woman,' said Betch. 'I think it was going to wait until your champion was defeated and laugh at you for not knowing you were doomed to failure with any man warrior you managed to free.'

Will looked at Jo.

'There *was* something especially nasty in the way the cat said that, wasn't there?' he said.

'It's elementary, my dear Betch,' said a statue of a man in a tweed cape, a deerstalker hat and a big pipe in his hand. 'We need a female warrior.'

'Boudicca's as frozen as the other warrior statues,'

said a voice from the back of the crowd.

'Yes,' squeaked another voice. 'Even if you're right, we're still out of luck. There's no one like that in London, and even if there was, they'd be cursed to stick to their plinths like glue.'

Will looked round the circle of gloomy faces and slumped shoulders. Only Betch was smiling.

'What?' he said. 'Why are you still smiling?'

'Doesn't cost anything,' said Betch. And then he winked at Jo.

'What?' she said, looking at Will. He shrugged.

'Well,' said Betch. 'You know I said I had a weakness for girls furnished and burnished by the sun: Golden Girls?'

All the other statues had stopped talking and were leaning in to listen to what the shabby poet was saying.

'Well, you know what I like even more?'

'Er . . . no,' said Jo.

'I like Golden Girls called Joan. Wrote a poem about one once upon a time. One of my best.'

Jo winced. Will knew she hated being called by her full name.

'I'm not a Golden Girl—' she began.

'I know,' he said. 'Not on the outside, anyway.'

'It doesn't make sense,' said Jo.

Betch stood up, his face suddenly serious.

'It does if you need a warrior who's also a girl, or a woman rather, a woman who's a fully armed and fearless fighter.'

Jo felt relief. For a moment she'd been sure he was speaking about her. But she wasn't fully armed with anything except a sore knee and a walking stick

'That still don't make sense, Betcher Man!' said Tragedy.

'There's no one like that in all of London,' said Ariel, hovering above them. 'And even if there was—'

'I know,' said Betch. 'How fast can you fly?'

Ariel looked wrong-footed by the question.

'Very fast,' she said. 'None faster. Why?'

Betch looked down at Jo and Will.

'Either of you speak French?' he asked innocently.

Will looked at Jo.

'I'm doing it at school,' she said. 'Why?'

'Because we need a hero. And I know where to find just the girl.'

He pointed.

'In Paris.'

'What?!' said Will and Jo as one.

And when he told them not only what, but where and whom, the mumbling began again and a crumbling old statue of a medieval king spluttered forward and said,

'Her? But she's the LAST person who would come to our aid. And who could blame her!'

Jo looked at Will.

'What do you think?' she said, and the way she said it lifted his heart, because she looked at him and spoke to him as if his opinion was the only one in the whole crowd that mattered.

'I think if you send a thief to catch a thief, then maybe the same thing applies to Joans,' he said with a tight grin.

'I know what I think too,' she said. 'I think she IS the last person who would come and help us. So that's why I'm going to ask her. Because this is the last chance.'

'I'll come,' he said

'I know,' said Jo. 'But don't. You can't speak French. Stay here and see if you can come up with a Plan B. At the very least see if you can spy out what the cat's got planned for a champion. I think you should sneak back in and scout things out with Filax.'

The dog barked enthusiastically.

The Clocker leaned forward and coughed apologetically.

'I will accompany you. Museum source of time problem. Should see it myself.'

Will nodded and swallowed. Having the Clocker along definitely would make it less daunting somehow. But . . .

'We said we wouldn't be split up,' he said to Jo. She was zipping up her jacket.

'We aren't,' she said. 'We're working together. Just in different places.'

He took a breath and nodded.

'OK then. Wait a minute.'

He fumbled at his watch and handed it to her. It was one his dad had given him, with a compass attached to the strap.

'Take this,' he said gruffly. 'Go on. The compass'll help you . . . you know, find your way home.'

'I know where we're going,' said Ariel briskly. 'She won't need that.'

Jo took it and strapped it to her wrist. She nodded her thanks.

'Meet you at the museum before sunset,' she said.

He nodded, trying not to show how much he suddenly didn't want her to go.

'*Bon voyage.*'

'Smart-arse,' she said, and with a brief wave and an

even shorter smile she followed Ariel into the sky and headed south.

# 12

## Better Than Nothing

The Sphinx knew it had made some kind of mistake in taking the woman to Bast. It was not hostile to people, not really. After all, being half human, half lion meant it had a shouting interest in both sides. But its sense of mischief and the small sliver of malice at its core had spent itself.

It was as if the act of doing rather than saying something nasty had, for the moment at least, purged it of its habitual discontent and misanthropy.

And now the Sphinx felt bad. It felt worse knowing it was its own actions that had led to this unfamiliar feeling. And there was something in the frozen human faces that didn't sit well with it.

So it was walking past the high wall of Buckingham Palace gardens feeling less regal than normal, on a probably forlorn quest for atonement. The Sphinx didn't know if it would feel better not doing anything, but it suspected it was better to try.

The traffic around Hyde Park Corner was as thick as ever, but since it was not moving, the giant statue was able to weave through the buses and taxis and walk on under the high stone arch of the Quadriga. It only stopped when it got to the War Memorial. And when it was there it looked at the statues, willing one of them to look back, but they – being soldier-statues – were as unmoving as the pedestrians dotted around the grass and the paths that crossed it.

'I may have done some harm, Gunner,' said the Sphinx to the tough-looking statue leaning against the stone plinth with its tin helmet tipped low over its eyes and its arms spread wide under a rain cape. 'I may need some . . . help. If things change. And if you are free to move again. I'm sorry for this. It's going to be . . .'

The Sphinx looked into the sky as if the word it was searching for might be found hovering just overhead.

'. . . undignified.'

And with that it leaned down, took the Gunner carefully in its teeth and lifted him off the plinth.

Then it turned and began to walk slowly back towards the distant museum like a depressed dog carrying a rather lumpy and warlike stick.

# 13

## A Bad News/Good News/
## Bad News Kind of Thing . . .

It had all been going so well. The Clocker and Will
had followed Filax back to the museum without
being spotted or attacked by anything nastier than
the growing sense that all the frozen people they
jogged past were turning into a much too familiar part
of the cityscape. Will realised he was thinking about
them as objects to be avoided, like statues or
street-furniture, not as real people with lives of their
own; they were becoming too close to a permanent
feature for comfort.

Part of this feeling was increased by the fact that
blue hoarfrost that seemed to be a by-product of the
freezing curse was getting thicker, so their faces were
becoming less distinct and individual as the ice-like
stuff thickened their features and began to erode their
individuality.

'If this goes on much longer they're going to look

like stalactites,' he whispered as they slowed and crept towards the loading dock hidden away in the nether regions of the museum, where a long crate was conveniently being carried through the open door by two motionless delivery men.

'Stalagmites,' said the Clocker. 'Other way round. Sorry. Pedantic.'

Will didn't exactly know what pedantic meant, but he just grunted and ducked through the door behind Filax.

'Be a job to get things moving,' said the Clocker. 'If succeed. Cat lifting curse will not make them move. Will only lift obstruction to putting things right. Will be my job to put time back in joint. Will happen slow. Like ice melting. Longer they frozen, longer to get moving again. But I can do it. No fear. If curse lifted.'

Will didn't feel like talking. Actually, what he most felt like was sleeping, but that was not about to happen any time soon as far as he could see. He carried his mother's scarab bracelet in his hand like a set of worry beads, pressing his thumb painfully into the sharply cut side of the scarab to keep himself alert.

He hoped Jo was OK, and consoled himself that

she was being led by Ariel, who was if nothing else a good flier and would look after her. He hoped.

He was getting woozy-headed with exhaustion, and had to stop bumping into things as they made a slow advance through the maze of passages and storerooms beneath the museum. He knew on any other day, in any other circumstances, that he would have been fascinated by all this behind-the-scenes stuff. He knew he was making a once-in-a-lifetime journey through the bowels of a real treasure-house, full of usually hidden objects. It should have been fascinating, but it wasn't. Everything was an obstacle, and every corner or door might hide the horrible thing that could jump out and attack them

Filax carefully led them forward then up a couple of flights of stairs, sniffing as he went.

'His nose a good alarm,' whispered the Clocker encouragingly. 'Hard for almost anything to hide from a dog's sense of smell.'

Will allowed himself the luxury of feeling a little cheered by that thought. And the cheer lasted all the way round the next two corners and through the door that led towards the back of the great glass-domed expanse of the inner courtyard.

It lasted all the way up until the moment the

dragon stepped out of the shadows and blocked them with its shield.

'Oh,' said the Clocker as the three of them went very still.

Dragons were clearly one of the few things Filax's nose could not warn them about.

The dog growled, low and threatening.

The dragon looked over its shoulder, obviously looking for reinforcements, clearly about to raise the alarm.

Will prepared to run.

Then the dragon turned back and held up a single talon to its mouth – almost as if it was warning them to keep quiet.

Filax stopped growling.

'That . . . odd,' breathed the Clocker.

'Ook,' said the dragon.

'No,' said Will, relaxing. 'That's Farty.'

Relief crashed through his system, flushing the bitter tang of fear away. It was going to be OK.

'Hi, Farty!' he said, sketching a wave.

'OOK,' said the dragon, and he lunged forward, batting Filax to one side with the shield in his eagerness to snatch the bracelet out of Will's unsuspecting fingers.

'What?!' gasped Will. 'Hey, Farty, give it back, not cool . . .'

He'd spoken too loud. There was noise from the other side of the big curved building at the centre of the courtyard, the sound of grunting and talons starting to jog towards them.

The fear flushed right back into his system, washing away the relief in an instant.

Farty looked at them. He looked worried, not threatening. He flapped his short arms in an unmistakable shooing gesture.

'Oook oook oook!' he said urgently. 'Ook!'

He was telling them to run and hide.

Will didn't waste time trying to keep track of the roller coaster of emotions triggered by the dragon's seemingly contradictory actions.

The Clocker melted back into the passage, Filax went in the other direction and Will flew upwards.

He didn't remember deciding to fly; it was as if the helmet was thinking for itself. He was three metres off the ground before he thought of changing direction and following the Clocker, and by then it was too late as three more dragons and a pair of lion-headed stone warriors came running round the curve of the building to see what the noise was. He accelerated and slipped over the parapet on the top of the structure, where he ducked down and lay splayed against the roof with the glass dome just above him.

He lay there breathing hard as he tried to decipher what was going on by noise alone. There were some grunts and growls and some answering 'Oooks', as if someone was explaining away the noise, and then he realised he could use the glass roof as a mirror to see below, but all he saw were the dragons, presumably including Farty, walking away, and one of the warriors loitering by the passage in which the Clocker was hiding.

Of Filax there was no sign.

With the warrior still below him, there was little he could do for the moment. In fact, now that the dragon had stolen the second bracelet, there was little he could do at all.

So he just lay there and hid, thinking of how he'd come to be in such a ridiculous and powerless place at this worst of all times: they'd got into the museum without being spotted. Which was good. Then they'd been caught by a dragon. Which was bad. But it had been Farty, and no flames had been involved. Which was good. But Farty had taken the scarab bracelet on which all of Will's hopes for his mother's rescue seemed to hinge. Which was bad. But then he had not given them away to the other dragons or the wretched cat Bast. So . . .

. . . so as he hunched on the roof and yawned, fighting the tiredness that was trying to tug him down into a treacherous sleep, he reflected that it had, all in all, been a bad news/good news/bad news kind of thing, and the one thing he must not do to make it worse was fall asleep.

Which – thirty seconds later – is precisely what he proceeded to do.

# 14

## *Golden Girl*

Ariel flew very fast, towing Jo by the hand. To begin with, Jo had kept checking Will's watch as they streaked across south London, following the railway they had picked up beyond Blackfriars Bridge. She wasn't that worried about losing her way with Ariel navigating the steel rails ribboning towards Kent and the Channel Tunnel beyond, but the speed at which Ariel flew was so vertiginous, and the absence of anything familiar close by – like her brother – made her feel a little hollow and queasy. Focusing on the small compass as it bobbled on her wrist gave her something to do and distracted her.

The rails had led them out of the city and over the suburbs. London never really seemed to stop, and then, when she looked down again, it had, and they were powering over the gently rolling farmland and strips of houses that punctuated it. She had wondered if there would be a sudden lurch as the spell cast by the malignant Bast lost its power at the outer edge of London. She had worried that all other sorts of magic might stop at that point and she would find herself tumbling out of the sky with a pair of useless bronze sandals dragging her even faster towards a sudden fatal full stop on the ground below, but that didn't happen.

Everything was frozen all the way to the coast.

'It's all stopped!' she shouted, her words whipped away by their slipstream. 'Everywhere!'

Ariel looked round, her face shining in the early afternoon sun.

'What?' she shouted.

'I thought everything might not be frozen outside London,' she shouted back. 'I don't understand!'

Ariel shrugged.

'What's the good of understanding?' she shouted. 'It just is what it is. And we shall have to do with it *as* it is. Don't see it makes much difference anyway, does it?'

Jo watched her turn away and speed on, the wind howling past, riffling her hair and the wisp of material she wore instead of a dress, a wisp that was, as always, looking like it was about to blow off her, but never did.

She was about to carry on the conversation but her eye was caught by the approaching English Channel. The sea was glinting in the sun, a gunmetal bed of flatness that stretched across the horizon like a too-abrupt punctuation mark that ended the green patchwork of England rolling away beneath them and became something altogether more alien and serious the closer they got to it.

'How fast are we going?' she shouted.

Ariel didn't seem to hear her. She just bunched her muscles and leaned into the air ahead of them, picking up speed as she did so.

As they sped over the landscape Jo noticed something odd. The air seemed to get . . . thicker.

'What's happening?' she said.

Ariel pointed down. A cow looked slowly at them as they tracked across the sky.

'It's the edge of the curse,' said Ariel. 'It doesn't stop suddenly. Because everyone outside the curse would notice. But they don't. Time just goes slower and slower the closer you get to London until it just stops. So if you're moving towards London, it's like walking into an elastic bubble. Or treacle. People don't actually notice it's taking them hours to move an inch until they're not moving a bit. They think time's normal because in the little bit they're standing in, it is. Relatively.'

'I don't understand,' said Jo. 'It doesn't make sense!'

'It's a curse,' said Ariel. 'It's not physics. It doesn't have to make sense. It only has to *be*.'

She pointed at the traffic in a country lane.

'You watch. Things will start speeding up back towards normal the further we fly.'

Jo watched, and, just as Ariel had said, soon enough the world was moving at its normal speed and the air was no longer thick, as if they'd pushed through the edge of an invisible bubble.

'What happens when the curse is lifted?' she shouted. 'In London. If we win.'

'The Clocker puts time back in joint,' said Ariel, as if that explained anything.

The sea was upon them much sooner than Jo had anticipated. She hadn't had time to think what it would be like to be flying over such a featureless and unfriendly expanse of water, but now it was right in front of her she stared down at it and worried about falling. And perhaps because the view beneath her feet was so repetitive she found herself yawning.

'Just close your eyes and leave it to me,' shouted Ariel, who'd been watching her.

'I'm fine,' said Jo, shaking her head to wake herself up.

The only thing that could make this whole flying thing even crazier would be falling asleep, even if she could, which she knew she couldn't. And she didn't need any more crazy in her life.

That was one thing she was sure of.

She fought to keep her eyes open.


The next thing she was sure of was that they were decelerating rapidly, and that she was cold and that she should open her eyes and wake up.

And when she did the Channel was gone and they were flying over the roofs of a very different city than the one they had left . . . how long ago?

'I nodded off!' she said in disbelief. 'I can't believe I did that.'

'You slept like a baby,' said Ariel, angling their approach along the wide river below. It was a chalky green, quite different to the muddy brown of the Thames.

The familiar silhouette of the Eiffel Tower passed on their right.

'But you snored like an old man.'

'Did not snore,' yawned Jo, rubbing her eyes and

trying not to miss a single detail of the city around her.

'Did,' said Ariel. 'Was probably the slipstream, but you definitely snored. Wasn't awfully ladylike.'

A bridge whipped beneath them and Jo saw that the statues here were not the dark bronze of the London statues but exuberantly gilded confections, explosions of gold that glistered in the sunlight. She saw a soaring Pegasus and any number of almost-clad maidens whip past below them.

Then she noticed the obvious thing she had missed for a moment. Here, in Paris, no one was frozen. The city was moving like normal.

'They're moving,' she shouted.

'I noticed,' said Ariel.

A horrible thought hit Jo.

'But they'll see us!'

Ariel brought them in to land close to the river, on a traffic island. No one paid them a bit of attention.

'Did you see a statue move before this happened?' said Ariel. 'Did you see unLondon?'

Jo shook her head.

'That's right,' said Ariel. 'We're impossible, and the human mind protects itself by not allowing itself to see the impossible. So, trust me. No one's going to see us. We're in unParis. And that's who we've come to see.'

She spun Jo round and pointed.

'You'd better do the talking. She's very proud and probably would be jealous of my grace and beauty. She's a bit of a tomboy but she's still a girl, after all, even though she's wearing trousers.'

She squinted.

'Metal trousers, from the look of it.'

Jo stared across the street.

And there she was on a high plinth in the middle of the road, in the shadow of a looming old hotel building, a simple, serious-eyed girl, bare-headed but in full battle armour, on a gold-armoured horse, carrying a sharp lance with a long pennant cracking in the wind above her.

'Joan of Arc,' breathed Jo. 'OK. I get it.'

Jo could see why Betch was clearly besotted with her. It was impossible to see her and not feel her strength and her resolution. This was a kind of beauty that had nothing to do with being pretty or sexy: this was the beauty of a strong woman who believed in something worth fighting for.

Jo only hoped what she was going to ask for would fit that bill.

It didn't start well.

The Golden Girl had seen her arrival, and clearly

didn't like what she saw, because she geed her horse and leaned back as it leapt off the plinth and crashed to the ground.

Just as Ariel had said, the crowds moving around them didn't pay any of this a bit of attention.

Joan prodded her horse forward and pointed the lance – the very pointy lance – right at Jo as she advanced on her.

'Who are you?' shouted Joan, in French.

Jo leaned on her stick and raised her other hand, palm open in what she hoped was the sign of peace.

'I just want to talk,' she replied, hoping her French was good enough.

The horse and lance kept right on coming.

'Who are you?' repeated Joan.

'Jo,' she replied. 'Just Jo.'

'Jo is not a girl's name. You are not a boy! Who are you?'

She really was quite aggressive, and the horse was getting uncomfortably close.

'I'm Joan. Like you. Joan called Jo.'

'You are not French!'

'No,' gulped Jo, eyeing the lance. 'I'm er, British.'

'British!' hissed Joan. The horse lurched forward.

'Stop!' said Jo.

The Golden Girl pulled back on the reins and stood in her stirrups at the very last moment, almost as if she was stamping on the brakes in a car.

The horse snorted, ducked its head and came to a halt, nose to nose with Jo, who hadn't stepped out of the way.

'Who are you, British, to stop me!' barked Joan of Arc, the pennant on her lance cracking in the wind over her head with a sound like rifle shots.

'I'm no one,' said Jo, looking up at the armoured statue that now loomed above her like a spiky four-legged tank. 'I'm just another Joan. Just another girl, trying to save the things she loves. Just like you.'

Joan reined in the horse and sat there, watching her through narrowed eyes.

'You're nothing like me, Joan-called-Jo. You come from England. I hate the English. You can barely speak French. I fought the English. They betrayed me. They hurt me.'

'I didn't,' said Jo. 'And that's history. This is now.'

'Why do you walk with a stick?'

'Because I have to,' said Jo. 'Not because I like it. Why are you on a horse?'

Joan looked surprised.

'Because I am a soldier,' said Joan.

'What do you fight for?'

Joan indicated the whole of Paris with one theatrical sweep of her lance.

'This. I fight for what is good, and right, and beautiful.'

'Well,' said Jo. 'That's what I want to ask you about . . .'

And there, as the busy city went about its business, oblivious to them, Jo told her story in her halting French, while the Golden Girl stared at her in growing incredulity.

'But you're English,' she kept saying. 'I am French.'

And Jo kept trying to tell her that right was right whatever nationality people were, but Joan kept shaking her head in disbelief.

Eventually Jo got angry.

'Look,' she snapped. 'History is water under the bridge. That was then, this is now, and what matters, what gets things done is working together.'

It was something her dad said. It made sense in English. She hoped she hadn't mangled it in French.

Joan stared at her. It was clear that, as angry as Jo was getting, Joan was becoming equally offended by the ridiculous request.

'Anyway,' she said, gesturing with both hands, 'how

could I help you? How could I fly? I do not fly. This horse has no wings!'

'No,' said Jo. 'But that's just an excuse. If you want a horse with wings, I just flew over a Pegasus that's easily as big as your horse.'

The Golden Girl stared at her.

'You don't give up, do you, Joan-called-Jo?'

'No,' said Jo, meeting her gaze and not blinking. 'Not when I'm trying to save my mother. And my brother. And a city full of blameless people – blameless people of all nations, by the way. But if you're too scared or proud to help people in trouble – well, just say so. It's not what we're taught about you in the history books, but who says the books are right? Maybe you like tyranny, maybe you don't mind innocent people getting hurt . . .'

There was a long, long silence.

'You know your trouble, Joan-called-Jo?' said the Golden Girl. 'You talk too much.'

# 15

## *Betrayal by Combat*

From his vantage point on top of the building in the centre of the courtyard, just below the hole in the glass roof, Will was able to see two things at once. The first was the light beginning to die into the pink of an early sunset outside, and below him a sudden scurry of movement among the frozen figures and animal statues below. The frozen people didn't move, of course. It was the animal statues moving out of the way as the giant stone scarab carrying Bast emerged from the Egyptian Gallery, guarded by the six cat-headed warriors.

Will felt a sick lurch in his stomach. He'd known time was running out, and that in fact it would run out if Jo was unable to get back in time, but he hadn't prepared his mind for what he'd do in that worst of all cases.

Bast paused in the centre of the courtyard and examined the dome of wildfire caging the Temple Bar dragon, like someone enjoying a pet.

The dragon snarled but was unable to do anything more. Bast purred with pleasure.

NO ONE LIKES A BAD LOSER, she said.

And then she arched her back and looked at the great glass dome above. Will ducked, sure that the cat was looking at him, but Bast didn't see him. She was looking at the light.

ALMOST SUNDOWN.

She sounded torn between irritation and elation.

THEY HAVE FORFEITED THE CHALLENGE. THEY MUST COME AND SUBMIT TO ME.

'Ah. No. Apologies. Not quite sundown,' said a familiar voice. Will peered over. No one was looking at him. Everyone and everything that could move was looking at the Clocker, who walked calmly out of the corner of the courtyard from where he'd been hiding behind the totem pole.

WHO ARE YOU?

'I am the Clocker,' he said with a curt bow that set all his dangling appendages a-jingle. He straightened and pointed to the sky. 'My curse to keep eye on time. And here to tell you it is not. Time. Not yet.'

BE STILL! howled the cat, and hissed a bolt of pure blue light at him. The Clocker didn't freeze or even

164

falter, just kept smiling and walking forward, a polite smile on his face.

BE STILL!!!

A second bolt had equally little effect.

'Cannot curse me,' said the Clocker, almost apologetically. 'Already cursed. Oldest curse takes precedence.'

WHAT ARE YOU?

'Told you. Timekeeper.'

Bast stared at him, her back arched, tail lashing.

IT IS TIME.

The Clocker looked at the sky again.

'No. Is only nearly time.'

He seemed entirely unconcerned with the sharp weapons the cat-headed warriors were pointing at him. He cleared his throat and checked one of his dangling pocket watches.

'Ah, but if anything to happen? Agree now the moment.'

Will knew from the raised tone of his voice that the Clocker was speaking to him.

And maybe it was, in the end, a good thing that he had not really planned for what he would do if the worst case arrived, because if he'd given it too much thought he might have not done what he did next.

Which was to stand, put his fingers in his mouth and produce the most ear-splitting whistle he could manage, another trick his dad had taught him.

Every eye that could move turned towards him.

'Right then,' he said, trying to keep the nerves out of his voice. 'Let's do this.'

It was also a good job he had the helmet to fly with, because he was pretty sure his legs were too shaky to bear his weight as he stepped over the parapet and hovered down, closer to the cat and its evil-eyed bodyguard.

As he floated down he saw Filax moving stealthily through the crowd towards the cat. Will caught his eye and shook his head. The dog would go down fighting if he had to, but this wasn't his fight. Will had this to do for himself, for Jo and for his mother.

YOU WERE IN HERE ALL THE TIME? spat Bast, looking accusingly at the bodyguards.

Will pointed at the hole in the roof.

'No,' he said. 'I just dropped in. Like we agreed. BEFORE sunset.'

He was now definitely in the zone marked 'making it up as you go along', but it occurred to him that the longer he could spin things out, the more chance there was Jo might arrive with a better plan. Or a champion that might actually win.

YOU ARE GOING TO FIGHT THE MIGHTY SEKHMET? said the cat. It was hard to see how such a small statue could inject such a massive quantity of gloat into a mere eight words. YOU?

'A deal's a deal, like you said,' swallowed Will. 'Me, or a champion, before sunset.'

WELL, I SEE NO CHAMPION. SO THIS WILL NOT TAKE LONG, said the cat. FOLLOW ME. THE ARENA HAS BEEN PREPARED.

Will had no choice but to follow along as the cat was carried out of the tall front doors on to the pillared steps looking down on the wide expanse of stone that was the museum forecourt.

Any attempt to think clearly about what he was going to do was blown out of his mind by the noise and the spectacle that met his eyes.

The wide expanse between the museum and the street was absolutely rammed. Animal statues of every shape and size were jammed together around an inner square of open space that was guarded by a cordon of silver-painted city dragons who were using their shields to push the crowd back. It was clear the square was to be the 'arena' that Bast had spoken of.

TAKE YOUR PLACE, BOY, hissed the cat.

I SHALL TELL SEKHMET THAT NONE OF
THEM ARE TO KILL YOU. NOT BEFORE YOU
HAVE TOLD ME YOUR SECRET. NOT UNTIL I
KNOW WHAT THE POWER IS THAT GUARDS
YOU FROM MY CURSE!

Will was dry-mouthed with fear, not knowing what
to say or do now that the worst case had not only
arrived but was slamming shut on him. And then the
cat's words hit him and he turned in surprise.

'Hang on,' he said. 'What do you mean none
of "them"?'

The cat drove the scarab forward in a short lurch
that knocked into Will and sent him tumbling down
the steps into the open square below. He scrambled to
his feet, angry now.

'What do you mean by "them"? We said champion,
not champions!'

I SAID SEKHMET THE DESTROYER, WHO
NO MAN CAN BEAT, CERTAINLY NOT A
LITTLE BOY, said the cat.

'I may be a boy,' said Will, 'but I'm not a coward
and a cheat like you.'

The cat bared her fangs and hissed at him as if she
wanted to spring at his face. But then she stepped back.

YOU THINK YOU'RE BRAVE? THEN TEST

YOUR COURAGE AND MEET YOUR DOOM. SEKHMET, SHOW YOURSELF!

There was a sudden thunderous roar as the six lion-headed stone warriors who were Bast's bodyguards stepped forward and slammed the butts of their pikes on the ground.

TREMBLE BEFORE THE SIX FACES OF SEKHMET! HUNTRESS, PROTECTOR, AVENGER, THUNDER-IN-THE-NIGHT, SILENT KILLER AND GRINDER-OF-BONES.

As she reeled off their names they each roared louder, hard hate-filled stone eyes boring into Will like drills.

The noise was so loud it hit him like a hammer, and he swore he could see all the animals around him step back away from the force of it. And then he saw the Clocker dart forward, through the dragon cordon, and come beside him

'Look,' he said. 'Cat a cheat. Champions will hurt you. No shame in giving up. Tell secret. Don't have to fight.'

'Yeah, I do,' said Will quietly, hearing the strain making his voice hoarse. 'Don't want to, but you know what? I just do. Because if I give up and tell her about the bracelets, she freezes me and then has me *and* mum

– and Jo, wherever she is, *won't* give up. She doesn't know how to. She'll do something stupid and get hurt trying to save both of us, or worse than hurt and . . .'

In the end it was simple. He cleared his throat.

'. . . and she's my sister. She's the bravest, most stubborn person I know. So even if I have a million-to-one chance of stopping her having to face this, I'm taking it.'

'Boys,' said a familiar voice behind him. 'Always so . . . emotional.'

He turned to see Jo stumble into the arena. He saw she was totally exhausted and windblown by her long flight. She in turn was surprised by the strain on his face. He looked like he had aged a hundred years in a few short hours. The eyes of the waiting statues seemed to suck the last of the energy from her. She felt Will gently put his hand under her arm and keep her on her feet.

'Lean on me,' he said quietly. 'Just this once. Don't let them see you're feeling weak. Don't give them the satisfaction.'

She pulled herself upright and they walked forward towards Bast and the six Faces of Sekhmet, who flanked her like an honour guard.

YOU ARE THE CHAMPION? spat Bast in a tone that dripped derision. YOU? A GIRL, A *GIRL* COMES TO FIGHT THE MIGHTY SEKHMET, THE DESTROYER, THE ONE WHOM NO MAN MAY CONQUER?

'No,' said Jo, hoping her voice sounded confident. She cleared her throat. 'Or rather, yes. Yes. Me. Me and my champion. You said we could have a champion.'

WHERE IS HE THEN? roared Bast. WHERE IS THIS CHAMPION WHO WILL SOON BE SLAIN BY THE MIGHTY SEKHMET?

'Oh, he's not a he,' said Jo. 'Like you said, a man can't defeat Sekhmet.'

WHO IS THE CHAMPION? hissed Bast, staring around the yard.

'No one,' said a voice from above. 'Just another girl.'

Jo caught her eye, and just for an instant was sure she'd seen the very serious girl look back and drop an eyelid at her, but it happened so fast she wondered if she'd imagined it.

The animal faces looked upwards and Will saw that they all were touched by the golden rays coming from the sky: gilding manes, horns, muzzles, snouts, trunks, tusks and eyes alike. The glow did not come from the setting sun.

They came from the descending gilded Pegasus and the Golden Girl riding on its back.

Even Jo, who of course knew what was coming in to land in the open square, held her breath and forgot all her fear for a moment. She'd seen a lot of angels and Victory statues in the air over the last day, but she had never seen anything more like a real angel descending from the clouds than this armoured girl with her long lance and battle pennant flying in the wind, riding the great winged horse all the way to the ground, slow, stately and majestic.

Even Bast was silenced.

The Golden Girl's glow seemed to banish the blue rime of magical ice that had begun to frost over the people below.

She looked like more than an angel.

She looked like hope itself.

The six warriors surged forward down the steps and arranged themselves in a curving line around her landing spot, weapons at the ready, snarling with malice and anticipation.

Joan looked at Bast and raised an eyebrow as the Pegasus slowed its descent.

'Wait,' she said. 'Six of them against one of me? Six of them. Really? Six? That isn't fair!'

The lion-headed warriors smiled, showing a lot of sharp teeth, and turned to Bast, knowing what was coming.

I DO NOT HAVE TO BE FAIR! I AM BAST, MIGHTY BAST, RULER OF THE— WAIT! NO! WHAT ARE YOU DOING?!

Will and Jo saw everything, but it happened with such speed it was only afterwards, when they replayed it in their memories, that they were able to appreciate the accelerated elegance of what was happening:

The moment the Pegasus's hooves landed softly on the ground, Joan simply swung her leg over the saddle and flowed into the attack. She hurled the lance straight through the first warrior with such force that it impaled him to the shield of one of the city dragons, who stumbled backwards into the crowd with the strength of the impact.

As she let go of the lance, her other hand simultaneously drew her broadsword and she spun, crouched low to the ground. Both hands met on the handle as the blade blurred into a golden arc that scarcely seemed to slow down as it scythed through the four stone legs of the next two warriors in line.

It all happened so brutally fast that Bast could only

squeal in a smaller, much higher voice: WHAT ARE YOU DOING?!

Joan didn't pay any attention.

She just kept right on moving, despite the gold armour managing to flow gracefully as she continued to attack the next warrior.

This one had time to mount a counterattack of its own, swinging a weapon that was part pike, part war-club straight down towards her unhelmeted head. But instead of dodging the blow she met it head on, sweeping onwards with her broadsword continuing to move fluidly as the follow-through of her scything blow turned into her own overhead attack, chopping downwards at ninety degrees to the ground. Her counterstroke went straight down the centre of the pike, splitting it end to end like a reed. The force of her blade continued onwards, neatly cutting the warrior in half from head to toe, only coming to an abrupt stop when it hit sparks off the paving stones between its feet.

There was a stunned silence and everything in the forecourt went very still.

Bast actually squealed. WHAT ARE—

Joan, still fluid and surging like an unstoppable golden wave, just carried on unhurriedly, moving on into the fight, stepping neatly through the middle of a widening V-shape made by the two pieces of warrior as they toppled sideways to face the last pair of Sekhmets.

To their credit, they had moved fast, leaping to one side and taking up a defensive position between her and the Pegasus. They watched, weapons ready, as she calmly walked towards them, her free hand casually pulling a long dagger from where it had been jammed through the belt at the small of her back.

'So. Next time? Don't stand behind the horse,' she said.

They looked at each other. If this had been a cartoon there would have been a bubble that read '?' above their heads.

This wasn't a cartoon. Pegasus kicked backwards with hind legs like a pair of gilded piledrivers.

The warriors each took a massive hoof in the back that sent them flying forward as Joan simply knelt to receive them, arms spread to either side. Her sword went through the body of one, and the dagger through the other.

And that fast, it was all over.

She held the weight of both for a moment, almost, thought Will, as if just to show that she could, and then she stood tall, dropping her arms and dipping the blades as she did so, rolling the stone bodies away on either side of her.

WHAT HAVE YOU DONE? squeaked Bast.

'Won,' said Joan, putting her dagger back in her belt.

BUT YOU JUST . . . ATTACKED! WITHOUT SAYING ANYTHING!!

'I didn't come to talk,' she said, sheathing her broadsword and swinging back into the saddle. 'I came to do this.'

BUT . . .

'And I did talk. I told you six to one was unfair. As you can see that it was. I do not lie.'

I THOUGHT YOU MEANT—

'People hear what they want to hear,' she said with a shrug. 'Especially powerful people. And people who think they are powerful do love to talk, in my experience. Fighting's a nasty, brutal business. Always best to get it over with quickly.'

She turned and gave Jo a nod and half a smile.

'Will that do, Joan-called-Jo?'

Jo grinned back at her.

'I don't know how to thank you,' she began.

'Then don't,' said Joan. 'I ought to thank you for

reminding me I should be what I am for everyone, not just for the people in my city. We all work better when we help each other.'

Jo nodded.

'Thank you anyway.'

Joan grinned again, took one look round the forecourt at the crowd of stunned animals, the people dotted among them and the hollow square lined with city dragons. She pointed at the broken lion-headed warriors sprawled around her.

'Don't know how things work in London, but in Paris if statues are back in their place at midnight—'

'It's the same here,' said Jo.

'Good,' said Joan, lofting into the sky as Pegasus flapped his wings in steady, powerful downstrokes. 'Then I will sleep better tonight after what I have done today.'

And with a wave, watched by every pair of eyes in the crowd below, she flew off into the setting sun.

Or followed by every pair of eyes except one. Unnoticed by everyone else, a single city dragon was waddling furtively backwards towards the doors into the museum. As soon as he was sure he wasn't being watched he turned and ran inside. His talons skittered on the shiny stone floor as he slalomed between the blue-rimmed figures of the frozen Londoners towards the great dome of wildfire at the centre of the courtyard. He stopped in front of it and checked behind him to make sure he wasn't being followed. He was panting with the effort and the unaccustomed running.

On the other side of the wildfire cage a single eye looked a question at him. He bowed his head and held something out, pushing it through the fiery bars, grimacing at the pain of the flames but doing it anyway.

Back outside, Will and Jo stood together and watched the Pegasus get smaller and smaller with every powerful wing-beat as it carried Joan back towards the Channel.

'Good job,' breathed Will, squeezing her shoulder.

'You too,' she said, squeezing back. 'You too.'

'Can't believe we did it,' he grinned. 'But we did.'

And then they turned to look at Bast, who was glaring at them from where she was still perched on the giant stone scarab at the top of the steps.

'We won,' said Will as they walked towards it.

'Fair and square,' said Jo. 'No thanks to you. Now you have to give our mother back.'

The cat bristled with outrage.

NO.

They stopped and stared at the cat. She sat back and calmly began to lick her fur back into its customary smoothness.

'What?'

NO.

The single word hit them like a bullet.

'You can't just lie and cheat like that!' said Will.

I AM A GOD, said the cat with a definite smirk. I CANNOT LIE. I JUST CHANGE THINGS. IF YOU CANNOT CHANGE THINGS, WHY BE A GOD?

'But we beat you!' shouted Jo. She pointed at the fragments of broken warrior statue on the forecourt below.

CLEARLY NOT.

Jo and Will both became suddenly aware that the cordon of city dragons had moved and was closing in behind them.

'Jo . . .' said Will.

Behind the dragons they could see the lion statues moving in as a second line of attack.

NOW I HAVE YOU, boomed the cat, her voice back to its usual confident level. I HAVE YOUR SISTER. I HAVE YOUR MOTHER. YOU WILL SHOW ME WHAT POWER PROTECTS YOU

AND I SHALL ERADICATE IT. OR I SHALL START BY THROWING YOUR MOTHER TO THE LIONS.

Jo looked up. Will had the same thought, that they should fly away now. But it was too late. Some of the dragons had taken to the air and were hovering there, as if waiting to pounce on them as soon as they left the ground.

They didn't have a chance. They were well and truly locked in the last case, and someone had thrown away the key.

YOU CAN'T ESCAPE, purred Bast. YOU ARE SURROUNDED BY DRAGONS AND LIONS, EVERY ONE OF WHICH WILL DO MY WILL. NO ONE CAN SAVE YOU!

There was a sudden blur of stone and snarl, and Filax barrelled out of the museum doors, skidding to a halt between the children and the advancing dragons. His hackles were up and his teeth were bared. There was no mistaking his intent. He was going to protect them. The line of dragons stopped.

Bast chuckled in contempt.

KILL THE DOG. BRING THE CHILDREN.

The dragons didn't move.

Filax barked and growled even louder.

'Don't,' said Jo, putting her hand on the dog's collar.

'You don't have to,' said Will.

Filax shook them off and barked in defiance.

The dragons went wide-eyed and took a step back.

Filax took a step forward. Even the lions backed up a pace.

KILL THEM ALL!!! shrieked Bast.

The line of dragons didn't move.

The lions looked embarrassed.

There was a beat of silence.

Then Jo and Will heard a noise from behind them.

'Ooky-ook-ook?'

Their eyes met. They turned to look back at Bast.

The cat had not seen him yet.

'Farty!' said Jo and Will at the same time.

Farty waved. His arm was still smoking, but he didn't seem to mind.

And then the dragon standing behind Farty, the REAL dragon, the rangy, spiky, alpha-predator, totally-frightening-utterly-lethal-Temple-Bar-king-of-all-the-dragons dragon leaned forward over him and gently tapped Bast on the back.

Bast spun and then froze. Her voice dwindled to a squeak as the reality of the situation hit her.

WHAT . . . BUT . . . HOW   DID   YOU . . . BREAK . . . MY CURSE . . . ?

'Ook. Ook,' said Farty, smiling at Will and Jo, his red tongue lolling happily out of his mouth as his stubby arm pointed at their mother's scarab bracelet that the bigger dragon wore around his clawed talon.

The Temple Bar dragon roared into Bast's face.

The roar rang off the surrounding buildings and shook the ground beneath their feet. The roar blew the cat's ears backwards and though there was no flame, the cat looked flayed by the noise alone. She stood there shaking as the roar continued, and as it did so the children realised that the dragon was shouting something at the cat, something they could not understand.

When it stopped roaring, it blew a circle of multicoloured wildfire like a blazing smoke ring, and calmly reached up and tossed it over the cat, who found herself trapped in a ring of fire that neatly fitted the scarab's back.

The cat immediately hurled herself at the dragon, claws out, screeching in anger, unstoppable in her pure fury – until she bounced off an invisible wall and landed back in the middle of the fire ring. Shrowling in rage she clawed and threw against all angles of the compass, one after the other, with no better luck. She moved so fast she looked like a cat caught in a whirlwind.

BE STILL! BURN IN YOUR OWN FIRE! BE GONE, THIS MAGIC. I CANNOT BE CHAINED! YOU CANNOT! I AM BAST! MIGHTIEST B— YOU CANNOT!

The dragon barked at it again. It stopped dead. Panting.

And this time the Clocker stepped forward and translated.

'Dragon says: this not your city. This is London. City belongs to itself. Has always belonged to itself. And here, of all places in the wide world, a deal is a deal. Do what you promised or you will burn.'

Will stepped forward.

'Free our mother.'

The cat said nothing. She suddenly looked so bedraggled that she probably couldn't. Instead she turned the scarab and they followed it as it lurched back into the building and headed slowly for the Egyptian Gallery.

# 16

## *The Final Twist*

'Will,' said Jo as they followed the scarab as it wound its path through the frozen crowds within the museum. 'I'm worried about how Mum's going to take the shock.'

'I know,' he said. 'Same here.'

'Worried about you too,' she said. 'I mean, is it going to make us go mad if everything goes back to normal, but we remember things as they are now? You know, not just that the city and everything got frozen in time, but that these guys, the statues, that they're real. That they move and have lives that nobody in London can see?'

Will thought about it.

'I know what you're saying.'

'I mean, we probably won't go mad because we know it, we'll go mad with frustration or something, knowing it's happening but we can't see it.'

'Things change. Nothing's set in stone. Not even

stone. Or metal.'

She smiled. 'You showed me that. You helped Farty change, right? And that's what saved us in the end. One act of kindness. Maybe now we've seen the unLondon, we'll always be able to see it?'

'Won't that make us even madder?' said Will. He had thought he would feel relieved and triumphant now Bast seemed to be conquered. But he didn't. Or at least he didn't just feel that. He also felt sad, a sadness he could see was also gripping Jo. What they'd been through was a nightmare. But it was also an adventure. It was a view into a hidden world where a kind of magic happened, and knowing that the door that let them into that world was about to close, well, it felt like the end of something wonderful as well as something terrifying.

Mind you, he reminded himself that they weren't there quite yet as they approached the white-coated group frozen in the act of replacing the broken fragment that had started all the trouble in the first place. His heart lurched in happiness as he recognised the still figure of his mother standing by them.

As if to underline the fact that they weren't quite at the end, Bast had regained some of her former pride and nastiness. She turned to look at them, taking care not to touch any of the wildfire that imprisoned her.

THINK THIS WILL HELP? she hissed. I HEARD YOU. AND YOU ARE RIGHT. SHE WILL GO MAD WHEN SHE FINDS HERSELF TRAPPED IN THIS FROZEN WORLD.

'Then unfreeze it,' said Jo.

The cat purred.

YOU CANNOT MAKE ME DO THAT. THAT WOULD PUT ME BACK IN THE PRISON I HAVE ESCAPED FROM. SO HERE IS MY GIFT. A MAD MOTHER.

Before they could stop her, she hissed at the pool of blue light in the sarcophagus, and whatever the ancient words were, they had enough power to ripple the light and then spin it into a whirlpool that opened wide. Then it snapped shut with a sharp slap of water on water; a drop of it splashed into the air in a lazy arc that hit their mother on the shoulder.

She shuddered, sneezed and then looked round. Jo and Will started to run for her as one.

'Mum! It's OK, it's us, don't—' Will shouted.

She spun and shouted back at them, holding out a gloved hand in warning.

'Jo, Will – STOP!'

They jerked to a halt.

'Nobody move,' she said very calmly.

She didn't seem to have gone mad.

She seemed in charge.

Will and Jo exchanged a look that said neither of them had thought it would go like this. That neither of them knew what was going on.

'We can explain . . .' said Jo.

'Mum,' said Will.

'Just a second,' she said.

She turned and took a step towards the sarcophagus. Jo and Will were bowled aside as Bast, with a violent roar of panic, urged the scarab forward in a last ditch attempt to stop her.

Their mother spun round, eyes wide at the incoming attack. There was no room to avoid it. Just when everything had seemed headed for a happy ending, it all went horribly sideways. She was going to get run over, as if hit by a small angry car. Will and Jo, sprawled on the floor on either side of the passing scarab, must have seen it at the same instant, because without thinking they each reached out a hand and grabbed one of the stone beetle's hind legs, throwing themselves violently backwards.

It was unthinking.

It was an act of despair.

But it was teamwork.

And it worked.

The scarab stopped abruptly and tipped forward, before Will and Jo's combined strength yanked it up and backwards.

Bast tumbled off its back and landed in a very ungainly and un-catlike pile on the floor. The ring of wildfire also fell with the cat, still surrounding it. The scarab went still, as if its power had died.

Will and Jo's mum saw this and, in one very precise move, reached over the white-coated museum technician frozen in the act of replacing the broken fragment on the sarcophagus, and twisted it out again.

There was a flash and a pop as the spell broke, and the blue light running round the band of hieroglyphics that it had once completed spilled out of the break and onto the floor.

NOOO! howled Bast.

Will and Jo's mother stepped back and carefully dropped the fragment on the floor. It split into two unequal halves. She picked up the smaller one and then straightened, watching the spell reversing itself.

The light was almost solid and flowed like water, moving faster and faster as it accelerated across the floor and headed for the cat.

Bast leapt for the door but was met by another wave of blue light coming in the other direction.

A noise like a rising sight filled the room, and all over London the blue rime and the blue light began to drain from the city and flow its way along the streets and pavements back towards the very centre of the curse – which was, of course, Bast herself.

NOOOO!!! she howled as the blue light sucked back into her body, assaulting it from all sides as if she was a magnet or a black hole that pulled everything into itself.

And then, as the light thinned but continued to flow into her, a critical mass was suddenly achieved, and with a crack of something hardening she sat down suddenly and stopped moving.

And was, once again, just an ancient and unmoving statue of a cat.

Their mother nodded in satisfaction and looked at the small fragment of hieroglyph she was holding.

'Right,' she said with a bright smile. 'I think this should be taken away and lost. We don't want them trying to fix things again. Not everything that is broken should be mended.'

She stuck it in her pocket and opened her arms wide to receive the two laughing children, who hurled themselves into her arms.

Hugs are difficult to do justice to in words. Hugs are better in real life. But this was a long one and a fierce one and it was the best one any of them had ever had.

Eventually Will had to ask.

'Mum . . . how did you know what to do?'

'Yes,' said Jo, her voice muffled because her face was still buried in her mother's neck. 'How did you know how to break the spell?'

Their mother pushed them back and looked at them.

'Oh, the Sphinx told me,' she said, as if this was perfectly normal. 'I tried to do it earlier but that wretched cat froze me again.'

'But how—' said Jo.

'But why—' said Will.

There was a cough from behind them.

'Er, yes. Was meaning to say. Scarab bracelets, powerful things, protected you from Bast's curse, yes?'

Will and Jo exchanged a look. Then they looked back at the Clocker.

'Yes,' said Jo carefully. It was clear from the way he was shifting from one foot to the other something delicate was on his mind and he didn't know how to broach it.

'And you were wearing the bracelets before Bast was freed and froze the city?'

'Yes . . . ?' said Will.

'But you never saw any statue move before that?' said the Clocker, waving a hand in a wide swathe that took in all the watching statues around them.

'No,' said Will and Jo together.

'So might conjecture it not the scarabs that made you able to see the layer of unLondon you now able to see? Might think it something different that allows you, normal children, to see what others can't, yes?'

'One might,' said their mother, grinning (maddeningly) at him as if he was an old friend. 'If they were.'

'Mum?' said Jo carefully.

'I was frozen, love. Not normal.'

'What?' said Will.

There was a sudden clatter of hobnailed boots behind them and they turned to see the tin-hatted Gunner statue the Sphinx had carried there run into the room and skate to a halt, pistol in hand.

His level eyes took in the scene and he relaxed, holstering the weapon.

'She's never been normal,' he said. 'She's always been able to see us.'

And in stunned amazement they watched their mother jump up and hug the statue.

'Gunner,' she said. 'Oh, Gunner!'

'Edie,' he said. 'I came as fast as I could, once I could. Sphinx tried to make amends . . .'

'It did,' she said. 'At least, it warned me and told me what to do. But none of that would have worked if Jo and Will hadn't saved us.'

She beamed at her children over the big statue's shoulder.

'They saved London too,' Edie said.

'Of course they did,' grunted the Gunner, as if it was entirely natural. 'Little acorns, you know?'

'They look exhausted,' she said. 'But very happy.'

Jo and Will were happy. Will thought of the cold, grim fear he'd felt just before Jo arrived with the Golden Girl. It was precisely the opposite of the warm feeling beginning to flood back through his veins.

'Jo saved me,' he said.

'Will saved me first" she said.

They grinned at each other, sharing the same smile, maybe because they were both having the identical thought: though they didn't know exactly what was going on, right now one thing was rock-solid and certain: whatever had once been broken between them was mended.

The Gunner held their mum, Edie, at arm's length and grinned.

'And you look wonderful too, girl. Even your hair . . .'

'And you look just the same,' she laughed, and hugged him again. Will and Jo's mother's smile was like the sun coming out. But they both were still too confused to fully enjoy it.

'Mum?' said Jo. 'Er, he knows your name. How can . . . what . . . we don't . . .'

Their mother looked at them and grinned.

'Well, whatever gave you the idea you were normal either?' she said.

'Mum,' said Will, with a sense that where he'd been worried about a whole new door opening in front of them, an even bigger one had been flung open behind them. 'What do you mean we're not normal, and how come you know all these statues?'

She came over and hugged them again and then nodded towards the exit.

'We should let the Clocker put time back in joint,' she said. 'Look at the beautiful light in the sky out there. It's going to be a good day tomorrow, thanks to you two.'

Will and Jo stared at each other, then back at her as they moved through the crowd of still-unmoving people. They both felt they were going to burst with frustration and happiness at the same time.

'*Mum!*' said Will.

'How can you have always been able to see all this and never told us?' said Jo.

Their mother gave them each a powerful squeeze and her most – in the circumstances – infuriating, mischievous smile. It made her look like a girl herself.

'Everything in its own place and time,' said the Gunner, walking beside them, his hand resting companionably on Edie's shoulder, just as casually as if he'd known her all her life.

Edie darted her head left and right, planting a big kiss on each of her children.

'You'll get over the shock. Everything's going to go back to normal once the Clocker's done his thing and people start moving again. Normal for everyone else, anyway. You two? Your world's just going to be a bit bigger, that's all.'

She led them down the wide steps into a forecourt now nearly empty of animals and dragons, who were all now heading home. The hoarfrost covering the frozen people was also fading rapidly.

'I was shocked by it once, when I was lots younger than you, a long, long time ago,' said Edie as she led her children onwards, towards the rosy light of the evening sky.

'But that's another story . . .'

If you liked *Dragon Shield*, then you'll love *Stoneheart*! Set in the same world, George finds himself plunged into a world he doesn't understand after he breaks a carving in the Natural History Museum . . . Read on for a sample . . .

# 1

# BELLY OF THE WHALE AND THE MONKEY'S TEETH

George never spent any time wondering why he wanted to belong. He just did. Things were like that. You were in or you were out, and in was a lot safer. It wasn't the sort of thing you questioned. It was just there.

On the class trip before this one they'd been to the War Museum and learned all about trench warfare. George had thought that's what life felt like: just keeping your head below the parapet so you wouldn't get hit.

Of course that was last year, in the past, like all the other things about being a kid. He still thought about them sometimes. He still remembered what being a kid was like. But he was over that. He was twelve. Real Twelve, not 'Only Twelve', as his father had called it the last time they'd spoken. He knew *his* twelve wasn't anything like his dad's because he'd seen pictures of his dad as a kid looking clueless and speccy and fat, all of which – in George's twelve-year-old trench – would be the equivalent of sitting on top of the parapet with a big round target painted on your head yelling, 'Cooee, over here'.

George could remember talking and laughing about stuff like that with his dad, before his dad moved out and there was too much talking altogether.

He didn't say much at home any more. His mother complained about it, usually to him, but sometimes to other people late at night on the phone when she thought he was asleep. Somewhere inside it hurt when he heard her say that – not as much as when she said he used to have such a lovely smile – but nearly.

And nowhere near as much as never being able to say anything to his dad ever again.

The thing was he wasn't *not* saying anything on purpose. It was something that seemed to have just happened, like his baby teeth falling out, or getting taller. Mind you, he wasn't getting taller as fast as he would have liked, and right now that was part of the problem.

He was average height for his age, maybe even a bit more – but somehow he *felt* shorter, the same way he sometimes felt older than he was. Or maybe it wasn't exactly older, just a bit more worn and rumpled than his classmates – rather like his clothes. His clothes were all thrown in the same washing machine, colours and whites together, and though his mother said it made no difference, it did. It made everything pale and grey and washed out, and that's exactly what George felt like most of the time.

It was certainly what he felt like today, and not being able to see properly was making him feel more insignificant than usual; all he could make out was the whale's belly and the back of his classmates' heads as they clustered round a museum guide showing them something interesting. George tried to push forward, but all he got was an elbow in his ribs. He sidled round the pack and tried to get another view, careful not to push anyone.

He found a place where he could nearly hear and edged closer, peering through the thin gap between a circular stand full of pamphlets and a boy about four inches taller than him. As he rattled the stand with his shoulder and reached to steady it, the boy turned and registered him.

George found himself smiling at him on reflex. The boy didn't return fire on the smile. He just looked away without comment. George wasn't too worried about being blanked. In fact he was relieved. The boy was the name-maker, the one with the gift for finding the cruellest nicknames for his peers, then making them stick. He'd almost been a friend of George's when they'd all been new together, but finding his gift had given him a kind of easy invulnerability, a power that meant he didn't have to have friends any more, only followers. That's what made him dangerous.

The boy turned back round. This time he spoke. 'Something I can help you with?'

George froze. Then tried to hide the freeze with another smile and a shrug. 'No. Uh. Just getting a better—'

'Don't stand behind me.'

The boy turned away. But several others had seen, and in their eyes George saw something he recognized. Not interest, certainly not sympathy, not even much dislike. Just a pale gratitude that they weren't the target this time.

So George swallowed and stayed where he was. He knew enough not to be seen being pushed around. He knew once you did that you were sunk. He knew there was a level below which you couldn't afford to sink, because once you were down there, there was no ladder back up. Once you were in that pit, you were fair game for everyone, and everyone unloaded on you.

So he looked down at the square of marble he stood on and decided he'd stick to it. There were teachers present, anyway. What's the worst that could happen?

The boy calmly reached backwards and toppled the stand, right into George. He stepped back, but there wasn't enough room, so he batted at the metal column with his hands to protect himself. It hit the floor with a loud metallic crash, spilling pamphlets all across the tiling around George.

The room went suddenly very quiet. Faces turned. The boy turned with them, innocent-looking amazement quickly morphing into shocked surprise.

'Chrissakes, Chapman!'

The cluster of boys around him dissolved into hooting anarchy, and the three adults, two teachers and a guide, were left looking for the culprit. And with everyone else doubled up and pointing, there he was, head above the parapet, feet bogged down in a landslide of bright-coloured paper booklets.

Mr Killingbeck fixed him with a sniper's eye, crooked a bony trigger finger at him and fired a one-word bullet.

'Chapman.'

George felt his face reddening. Killingbeck snapped his fingers at the other boys.

'The rest of you clear Chapman's mess up! You – follow me.'

George walked after him as he stepped away from the mob.

He followed him out of the whale room back into the central hall of the Natural History Museum. Mr Killingbeck stopped in the middle of the room beneath the dinosaur skeleton and beckoned him closer.

George had enough experience of Mr Killingbeck to know not to start what was coming. So he just waited. The man's mouth worked slowly. He always worked his mouth as if everything that he said tasted bad, and had to be spat out before it caused him more pain and discomfort.

'Mmm, tell me, were you trying to be rude, Chapman, or does it just come naturally?'

'It wasn't me, sir.'

'Who was it then?'

There was no answer to that. No answer George could give. He knew it. Killingbeck knew it. So he didn't say anything.

'Moral cowardice and dumb insolence. Neither very

appealing, Chapman. Neither what you were sent here to learn, are they?'

George wondered what planet Killingbeck was on. Planet 1970-something probably. Not a planet where George could breathe. He began to get choked up. His face began a slow burn that he could feel without seeing.

'That was unforgivable, boy. You behaved like something wholly uncivilized. Like that ape over there.'

The bony finger jabbed at a monkey in a glass cage, baring its teeth in the grimace that would be the last message it ever sent to the world. George knew what it felt like.